Uesugi Kenshin

EIJI YOSHIKAWA

SHELLEY MARSHALL (TRANSLATOR)

www.jpopbooks.com

ISBN: 9781081600792

CONTENTS

Warring Dragon Flag Kanji

Bishamonten Flag Kanji

1
SIGNS OF LIFE

KENSHIN WOULD CELEBRATE his thirty-third birthday in the coming year.

Though still a young man, the colors of all his clothes and accessories were accurately described as subdued. His long-sleeved *haori* coat was a plain greenish-brown woven silk. Only his *oguchi-hakama*-style trousers seemed to be made of a special fabric. His head was always covered by his favorite *zukin* hood. Surrounded by a group of retainers dressed in fine, new spring clothes, he smiled and quietly surveyed them. From any viewpoint, he appeared to be a solitary young priest of the severe Rinzai school of Buddhism mingling with the group.

"Well, aren't my followers a foolish lot?" Kenshin began to speak to the man seated to his right.

Uesugi Norimasa, his adoptive father and the shogun's deputy in Kanto, nodded and said, "That's true."

Then nodding to the nobleman two seats away on his right, Kenshin said with a smile, "The wealth of courage and the patient strength in Echigo's masses will soon be heard about everywhere. No, it will be the first time they will hear about so many guileless, versatile warriors."

The lone nobleman among them was a court noble from the capital. He held the title of Lord Kumano but was Konoe Sakitsugu, an enemy of a senior regent of the emperor. During the great chaos under heaven in this year of Eiroku 4 (1561), on New Year's, this court noble somehow managed to drink sake while calmly peeking at the seats of only daredevil warriors to his endless delight. He found the men of the dojo who only understood the so-called beauties of nature to be a slightly different sort and imagined the great ambition in these warriors on a quest.

They had gathered in Umayabashi Castle in Joshu. It was located in a corner of the Bando Plain easily imagined as only being wilderness. In the very least, dignitaries of the time had to summon great resolve and purpose to travel to this place.

> Spring arrives, a dawn.
> An interesting world today,
> Like being born together now.
> A country stands alone.
> A country struggles alone.
> The clouds of last night disappear,
> A new sun rises and burns.
> Now is the age of the gods.
> Now warriors live again as ordinary men.
> Such is life
> Roots of the grasses are eaten.

The annual festive banquet was held on January 7. The young samurai of the Echigo force recited long poems in modern tones mixing in their provincial dialects. Finally, they rose in unison, crowded into the largest room while matching rhythms to form a ring and dance round and round. Today life was as enjoyable as it could be.

2

THE SHADOW OF SHINGEN

KENSHIN WAS STRUCK by a recollection while filling the cup of his father beside him and said, "New Year's every year is greeted with a military expedition like an annual festivity. Last year, the army was in Etchu. Where will it be next year?"

Uesugi Norimasa made a sour face and said, "I don't have power as a deputy who should be consolidating authority in Kanto. Being pressured from all sides, I have to rely on reinforcements from far away and cannot stand the shame."

Imagining the workings of his mind, Kenshin said in consolation, "I hear those words from you, but I can't see why you would say that. Don't take it so hard."

For a while, he was engaged in peace negotiations that started three years ago in the first year of Eiroku (1558) with his old nemesis Shingen of Kai. They were in the process of signing a friendship contract to be good neighbors in the future.

On the surface, the distress in the Echigo force was barely visible. As a result, when they engaged in battles, his hostility became negativity, and overall the situation became a struggle for Kenshin.

Shingen's political skills tunneled into the internal affairs of various provinces from his province of valleys and mountains. Above all, given his diplomatic foresight and wisdom, he absolutely should not have become an enemy in the head of the priestly general wearing a scarlet vestment, like the young Kenshin, who also accomplished great achievements after many attempts.

Last year, the campaign to Etchu was an attempt to crush the nuisance border raids by the Jinbou clan of Toyama Castle. When the remnants seemed to have been eliminated after the pacification, many among the soldiers spoke with the accent of Shinshu, the province bordering Echigo and

3

Etchu. Monk soldier disciples having the personal support of Shingen were mixed in among the soldiers. In time, the coming and going of countless secret documents were discovered. Evidently, this was the dancing shadow of Shingen.

This shadow was hard to contain. If one side was swept away, machinations emerged on another front. A rumor frequently heard in the world was Shingen had eight shadow warriors, *kagemusha*, and no one knew which one was Shingen. This may indicate the ever-changing appearance and disappearance of his tactical personality.

Last year, Kenshin rode out to Etchu and put down a disturbance at the border and returned to the daimyo's Kasugayama Castle. As soon as he extracted himself from his armor, he was contacted with an urgent demand to send support troops to Kanto from the Uesugi clan administering Umayabashi territory in Joshu.

The enemy was Hojo Ujiyasu of Odawara. The influence of Hojo often threatened the small provinces of Satomi and Satake. They reached the state in which the pressure was unbearable. Even after an appeal to the shogun's deputy Uesugi Norimasa, his actual ability to suppress had already been drained. If neglected, the turmoil would reach the area of Joshu and was a cry indicating danger to the independence of the clan in control.

Kenshin's consent was swift. He thundered down Mount Kasuga and pushed south to Joshu. These events occurred in August of the previous year. His grand plan for the conquest of Odawara was to make Umayabashi Castle his base and rally support from the small province of Boso. This plan was underway when spring was welcomed in this castle in Eiroku year 4.

By the fourth month of the campaign, the outlook of the war was still difficult to predict. If this battle were prolonged, sustaining morale would be essential. In times like that, poetry recitations were meaningful in eating up a great deal of time and in freeing the spirit. As he surveyed the scene, Kenshin looked satisfied. His guest Konoe Sakitsugu seemed to be enjoying himself. Only Uesugi Norimasa appeared to silently lament, Is this a good thing? and looked perpetually flushed by drink.

However, this banquet did not become rowdy. Each man understood restraint. The first men to dance and recite with the most debauchery were told, "Don't get carried away" and "This is enough" when served a cup. When the servers were encouraged to eat, each one took a large rice bowl and began to eat solemnly.

The noses of four or five comrades coming back inside had been turned red by the cold. They bowed to the lord and the guests from the lower-ranking seats then plunged into the crowd to grab chopsticks and rice bowls.

Kenshin spotted a man a distance away and called out, "Shimotsuke?"

Did he think he was being reprimanded? One among them, Saito Shimotsuke-no-kami, corrected his unsettled demeanor, bowed again and said, "Yes, I've just returned."

Kenshin said, "The rice will soon be gone. There doesn't seem to be anything left to drink over there. Come here," and invited him over with a cup.

3
SAITO SHIMOTSUKE

SAITO SHIMOTSUKE TIMIDLY advanced before the lord and the noble guest. Konoe Sakitsugu did not take his eyes off of him. He looked astonished and wondered if this sort of samurai existed in Echigo? In a word, Saito Shimotsuke could only be called an inglorious man. His left eye was shut, and he walked with a limp.

Still, Shimotsuke was a delightful follower to Kenshin, but he sat with extreme reserve opposite the nobleman who said, "Come closer," and offered him a cup.

Kenshin laughed as he scolded him, "Aren't you a big drinker? You almost missed today's golden opportunity when you slipped away this morning. You are a man with the usual big talk but lack a great accomplishment."

After Shimotsuke took the cup and drank all the sake, he answered, "The truth is, I returned from a visit to the tomb of my ancestor. I left at dawn and intended to return before the banquet. But I was delayed because I was unable to find the old trail buried under grass in an overgrown field."

"Oh, is that so?"

Kenshin instantly sobered up. A memory caused his eyebrows to stiffen. The ancestors of Saito Shimotsuke were not from Echigo. They were born in the village of Ikushina four to six miles east of Umayabashi Castle. Everyone knows that in Kenmu 2 (1335) during the days of pirates plundering Korea, the heavenly warriors of Nitta Yoshisada and his clan pledged loyalty and raised an army from villages that sprung from the plains of Jomo to strike at his long-time enemy Ashikaga Takauji in Kamakura.

After Kenshin left for Joshu, he went to that region a second time to mourn the soul of Yoshisada. He was unable to sleep at night without thinking of military campaigns. Were the loyal retainers of Kenmu enraged and roused from the weeds? Did they boldly take up the bows and arrows not seized by the enemy to finally die as martyrs for their country? He wandered the area having the raw product of growing grass, offered bitter tears from his heart to the many departed souls then returned. This second time, he built a small, temporary shrine in the area.

4

I AM YOUR MAN

FROM THE BEGINNING, Kenshin had a sensitive nature. He was easily excitable and oversensitive. He wept like a girl until he was nearly twenty years old. Around that time, not only his sensitivity but also his romantic side emerged in his personality. He abruptly entered Zen and aspired to train his heart to gravitate toward a complete change. He was born with a sentimental nature he wanted to keep and used Zen to not eliminate it from his blood. His fervor was raised and came to drive his future ambition. He cried over noble causes but not over small ones. Whether the issue was a serious provincial event or involved the name of a military family, he usually kept quiet. Most of the time, the area near his almond-shaped eyes smiled. His personality changed into one said to be unbecoming of a man in his prime.

In contrast, one could infer traces of long strides that pushed forward following his path and steadily advanced noiselessly to an ideal place. His most celebrated action was to go alone to Kyoto to give his New Year's greeting to the emperor at the Imperial Palace.

The distance between Kyoto and Echigo was longer than the distance from Hojo in Odawara, from Shingen in Kai, and from the Imagawa clan in Sunpu. However, Takeda Shingen, Imagawa Yoshimoto, and Hojo Ujiyasu were preoccupied with the offense and defense of his own province. Because neither one made a move yet, Kenshin quickly went to Kyoto while still a young man in Tenbun 22 (1553). Through Ashikaga Yoshiteru, the shogun at the time, he was received at the Imperial Court and presented with the emperor's gift cup and inspected various gifts. The significance of the bows and arrows taken by the retainer Kenshin was obvious to the world.

The year before last, Eiroku 2 (1559), he visited the capital again. Naturally, great happiness was often found in his loyalty even in the Imperial Court. However, Konoe Sakitsugu, a senior regent of the emperor, secretly worried about him. He asked, "You are absent from your remote land. Aren't

8

you worried about your native country?"

Kenshin answered, "Nothing is more important than a trip to the capital. It's nothing to leave a territory."

To the rival chiefs of various provinces under his sphere of influence, his first, frantic, bloodstained concern was those territories. The situation slipped into ferocious fighting over an inch of land. The regent Sakitsugu heard Kenshin's words and said, "I am your man," as he recognized the truth. This was expected. At that time, many lamented the moral confusion since the decade-long Onin War and the decline of the nation's customs neglected even in the ways of the Imperial Court and the vassals. Kenshin's words struck the heart of Sakitsugu. If he were a military commander, no matter what was disclosed to him or what great cause was entrusted to him, a written oath made using the *Kumano-goufu* talisman would later be exchanged, and the two would promise each other to act on behalf of the Imperial Court.

In anticipation of New Year's, Sakitsugu left the capital and came to this place, not for a superficial reason but for the connection of the hearts in their chests.

"Ah ... Is your ancestor a member of the Nitta family from this land?" Sakitsugu interrupted Kenshin and Shimotsuke from the side.

5

FAVORED BY THE ANCESTORS

SHIMOTSUKE HAD BEEN directly addressed but wondered whether a response was a good or a bad idea. To urge the awestruck man, Kenshin said, "Please answer."

Shimotsuke's one eye glanced at the nobleman and said, "I am humbled by your question. My ancestor Saito Kurando is not well known, but when Lord Yoshisada raised an army, he joined with Lord Wakiya of your clan and attacked Kamakura and later died in the Battle of Bubaigawara. I heard the tomb where his head is buried is in my hometown Takushi. I asked five or six natives to find out but no one knew a thing.... The fields and meadows have changed so much. Not one local peasant knew."

"So your family moved to Echigo several generations ago."

"It's been four generations."

Sakitsugu turned to ask Kenshin, "Oh, well then ... are many descendants of the Nitta clan in Echigo?"

Without having to think, Kenshin promptly replied, "Here, beginning with Shimotsuke, if there are five or six names, then there are tens of families in Kasugayama Castle who probably share the same lineage."

"Certainly. Certainly," Sakitsugu repeated then said, "To be an honored descendant is unimaginable. Forgive my earlier abruptness. Take this cup, Shimotsuke."

He didn't move forward but only reached out his hand.

The deeply moved Shimotsuke shrunk his body. He thought about his rank of nothing more than the samurai leader of a small squad of four or five men and seemed to be lost in thought.

"Take it."

Relieved after receiving permission from the lord, Shimotsuke raised his head and said, "I have done nothing to deserve this cup, but my ancestor's distinguished service can be considered. My taking one is too much. May I have all the cups to share with the other five or six names? After returning home, I will give them to the others in Kasugayama Castle.... May I?"

"Please do."

Sakitsugu took out his tissue to wrap the cups and handed them to Shimotsuke.

6
NAILED DOWN

PREPARATIONS WERE MADE. The governor-general's force gathering the soldiers of Jomo and Boso publicly denounced Hojo Ujiyasu based on Kenshin's orders.

"Surrender or perish," they chanted while advancing to the castle town Odawara.

From March to April of that year, the offensive and defensive war continued. Flowers scattered with the coming of spring.

Konoe Sakitsugu, a visitor at the front, said, "I secretly prayed for preparations for the great ambition in the world to come a day earlier for the sake of all four classes of society," then he returned to the capital.

When battles were fought, Kenshin saw him off as far as the Ashigara border.

"We will meet another time in the capital," he said with confidence and faith in a great future. However, Odawara Castle before him did not easily fall. The reasons were the rapid entry into the castle of the powerful military corps of the adviser Takeda Shingen from Koshu and the cooperation of Hojo Ujiyasu.

The adviser from Koshu stressed, "No matter how many times the lord calls on the military force and all levels of society to be the reserve force from Koshu, the wise plan based on this strategic point is to keep the focus on protection and never leave the castle gate to fight."

The attacking force was nailed down here. The Echigo force for military campaigns was exhausted. The plan for Kenshin was to do nothing.

The month of May came.

Not even a corner of the castle wall could be taken. The castle's plan could be said to be in its design. Finally, Kenshin withdrew his force. The ally's weariness was completely reversed, and upheavals among the enemy were awaited.

During this time, he made a pilgrimage with Uesugi Norimasa to Kamakura Shrine to the god of war. Norimasa took this opportunity to make this recommendation.

"In the future, I expect you to join my clan and take the surname of Uesugi."

Of course, until that time, Kenshin was a deputy to the shogun, carried the surname of Nagao, and held the post of the military governor of Echigo.

ASHES OF A DEAD LETTER

AT THAT TIME, the elite forces of Koshu frequently moved north either in formation or dispersed.

Of course, the movement of a large military force galvanized the surrounding regions. All the men and horses headed to Zenkoji Temple like scattered clouds along the Yatsugatake and Suwa trails. Infiltrators from Echigo who remained vigilant in this area were taken by surprise and failed to grasp the objective. But the moment they noticed, the general public also knew because the world's eyes were startled as if a thunderbolt flashed across a blue sky.

"Suwa is between Kai and Echigo."

The reason for the sudden rise of war clouds like cirrus clouds wasn't considered. Only terrors of the past were revived in the peasants.

This place was southeast of Lake Nojiri in mountains near the provincial border between Echigo and Shinshu and an important center of transport as a junction for the north, west, and south, and was a castle held by the power of Echigo by the impregnable steep pass of Warigatake.

It was Warigatake Castle.

The power here was equivalent to absolute for Echigo and valued greatly by the Takeda clan in Kai.

If taken by Takeda in the morning, the fate of the Echigo force must be to march east and seal all exits to the south. As long as the castle was under the control of Echigo, the Fierce Tiger Shingen of Kai would have difficulty achieving his future wish for expansion to coastal Japan north of Lake Nojiri.

The instincts of Kai and Echigo provinces always led to friction in this area. To capture or be captured, lives going to live in the south clashed several times with lives stretching to the north in several bloody battles like torrents meeting violently at the entrance to a gorge.

However, that destiny ceased four years before the first year of the Eiroku era. Peace was concluded through the work of the shogun Ashikaga Yoshiteru. Written oaths were exchanged, pledges were made to the shrine crest, and weapons put in storage. Then without warning, fires of war broke out at Warigatake Castle.

Oh no, not again? thought the public who had reason to be afraid. Their eyes and ears numbed as if struck by a thunderbolt because they were overconfident in their belief in a permanent peace between the two provinces.

GRIEF AND HOT SWEAT

"WHAT? WARIGATAKE?"

When Uesugi Kenshin received the initial report in the area of his current campaign, he shared the public's shock, like water had been poured into his sleeping ear.

He couldn't believe it but knew it was probably true. He had exchanged an agreement with Shingen and shared ideas on humanity.

In general, he was viewed as a young man brimming with an air of unworldliness, shining with intelligence and insight, and a diligent student of *The Three Strategies of Huang Shigong* and already possessing the ability of a famous general. His personality was not so valiant as to be unmoved by these views.

He burned with resentment. Out of character, the bloody color of rage boiled on his face and he cursed Shingen.

"Damn that Lord Long Legs!"

This was not a nickname given by Kenshin. Everyone called him Lord Long Legs of Koshu. He earned this name from his diplomatic nature and his drive. While in his province of steep mountains, he displayed a methodical fast pace and quick work.

However, Kenshin would not be outdone by the whirlwind of Shingen. Kenshin's speed was in his thoughts rather than his actions. He was determined to not wallow in regret when confronted with an obstacle.

"We'll withdraw immediately."

The men and horses under his command breathing hard and coated in sweat crossed three countries on their journey north.

"This is regrettable."

"Warigatake Castle fell in the end. All our allies died in battle with the castle's demise."

As he gasped for breath along the way, Kenshin heard this sad news from the reports that arrived one after another.

"I see."

He wiped the sweat away and looked up at the clouds resembling mountain peaks. The fiery sun scorched his tears of sadness.

"… I see," he said and continued the march in silence.

Seeing his anger and sorrow, the generals Naoe Yamato-no-kami, Nagao Totomi-no-kami, Ayukawa Settsu, Murakami Yoshikiyo, Takanashi Masayori, and Kakizaki Izumi-no-kami maneuvered their mounts to surround him but did not speak sternly.

There was only silence. They crossed mountain after mountain like clouds as they made a firm pledge about a simple matter on a later date. More detailed reports came.

"When the enemy captured Warigatake, they burned down the entire castle. When all traces of the stonewalls and the castle walls were gone, they quickly retreated to Koshu. The allies in the castle were destroyed, but enemy casualties were several times greater. Famous generals of the Koshu forces like Hara Mino-no-kami, Kato Suruga-no-kami, and Urano Minbu suffered injuries. Hara Mino-no-kami, in particular, was said to have retreated from this battle with thirteen serious stab wounds. The enemy's hatamoto Shinkai Matasaburo and Tsuji Rokurobei died in battle. I heard Tada Awaji-no-kami also died in battle."

The man with an urgent message gave Kenshin this detailed description of the war situation.

"Is that so?" was his surprisingly short answer. However, each time he spoke another word, the tone of his voice grew more solemn and muffled.

As the details were conveyed, a vivid tremor rumbled through the entire force. Perhaps, he was an old general on horseback who swallowed silent tears and used his fist to wipe away a spray of tears.

Grieving voices of retainers struck with emotion rose.

"What a shame."

"How awful."

From the porters and the ordinary men came questions like "Are we going back to Echigo like this?"

"Then this was all for nothing. We can't go back!"

Their sweaty faces blazed with spirit and grew in rage.

The dissatisfied grumbles from the officers and men throughout the force toward Kenshin were no surprise given that his silence was broken only by "Is that so?" If they faced west and looked from the summit of the mountain crossing, what looked like smoke above Warigatake resembled mountain peaks of clouds. When his whip was pointed to the left, Nojiri wasn't too far away. They could make a long drive and break through Kawanakajima, destroy the enemy base, capture Kaizu Castle, and occupy neighboring regions. They were not too late to take revenge on at least one end of Shingen's sphere of influence.

"What is this?"

They walked and walked and never stopped stamping the ground. Blood connected them to Warigatake Castle. The fathers of some men were there. For others, they were their brothers, uncles, and nephews. This solidified their connection to the name of the Echigo army and demanded justice for this betrayal by the Koshu army.

"Even from this place ..."

Their zeal quickened the chase.

"Stop the horses," said Kenshin to the generals around him as he turned his horse's head to the side.

9

THE BRIDGE IS FLOWING
THE WATER IS NOT

"STOP. SEND THE entire force west."

The order from Kenshin was relayed from one commanding officer to the next.

In an instant, they were engulfed by dust.

The meandering line managed to head west and lined up in silence.

All eyes near and far turned to the leader Kenshin.

"…"

Kenshin tucked the reins in his saddle seat and placed both of his palms on the horse's chest. He turned toward the western sky.

Every man from the senior generals and the hatamoto to the pack couriers at the distant end of the line sent secret prayers to follow him.

When he finished, Kenshin seemed to stretch up above his horse to recite a line from a Buddhist poem "The bridge is flowing, the water is not.… Forward! But first to our castle on Mount Kasuga."

The verse spoken loudly by Kenshin was not understood by many. They imagined it included words from Zen whose meanings they did not know.

"… the bridge flows, the water does not. Is that what I heard?" they asked and answered the question themselves.

But some understood.

"Water is something that flows but isn't flowing. That probably means it's eternal. If you thought it stopped, it flowed, and if you thought it flowed, it stopped. You can't see sorrow or joy right before your eyes. Isn't that what the lord said?"

For the time being, the expeditionary Echigo force entered Kasugayama Castle. Kenshin seemed to expect his life to return to normal once he was back at the castle.

The anger about Takeda's betrayal intensified daily in the popular mind throughout the entire land of Echigo and in the military from the generals on down. The monk Shingen could not be added to the line of a military family after the contemptible acts of simply ripping up the peace accord and taking advantage of Kenshin's absence during a campaign; he was a land pirate who did not reflect on the ordeals of peasants and townsmen. Even citizens of Echigo who were not warriors were grinding their teeth.

Nevertheless, Kenshin did not assume he would easily leave. Most of July had passed and August neared. When Kasugayama Castle was covered on and off by cicadas, Kenshin showed no signs of going on another campaign. Of course, the castle town's blacksmiths and providers of weapons, provisions, and munitions became active, but this wasn't strange at all for the Uesugi clan. All matters related to the military were commonplace.

"You must be patient."

"What happened?"

Even low-ranking samurai with little drive sometimes criticized his lack of focus. Later, they grabbed a man on his way back from the castle to ask, "Well,... how'd the talk go?"

He only answered, "Don't know," to his close associates who were able to read him.

"Today, too, the discussion was held inside with only clan members and senior vassals. But, as always, they had conflicts over war or peace."

Their witness didn't seem to know the truth.

However, feelings of both war and peace were felt among the castle commanders.

"What is peace? Even at a time like this, there's still room to consider peace. Coward!"

Hatred beyond the usual indignation grew fierce. And anger was heaped onto anger because they had no idea who should be the target of their anger. They only cried to Heaven.

Suddenly, the people in the clan unexpectedly found themselves ringed by suspicions. The figure of Saito Shimotsuke, who had not been seen lately, stood out with his one eye and his limp.

10
THE SECRET EMISSARY OF PEACE

WHEN FAMILY MEMBERS of Saito Shimotsuke were asked, "Where did Lord Shimotsuke go?" They sealed their lips. And the close friends who asked daily only had suspicions.

"I have absolutely no idea."

A peek into his residence revealed no signs that he was sick or asleep. The servants' lips were sealed. In this case, the natural state of the mind was the desire to know.

"I got it!" one man announced to a group.

It was already early autumn; August began a few days ago. The hatamoto Karasaki Zushonosuke came to the office in the castle. This man was the closest thing to being the passionate backbone among his comrades. He loudly announced, "I shouldn't know this, but he's the emissary for peace and secretly went to Koshu."

Their faces registered no surprise over this matter. More than amazement, they gasped and their eyes widened as if a huge rock were dangling above their heads.

"What? Is that true?"

"Do you think I would say something so serious as a joke?" asked the stone-faced Zushonosuke.

According to him, his uncle Kurokawa Osumi-no-kami also disappeared recently. The story was that he was ill, but Zushonosuke had doubts. He finally heard the truth by intimidating a young woman who was his cousin.

"So Kurokawa Osumi went with Saito Shimotsuke to Koshu?"

"It seems so. It's a secret, but Shimotsuke is called the senior envoy and Kurokawa Osumi, the deputy. They left Mount Kasuga ten days ago."

"… I didn't know."

"There was no reason for you to know. If leaked, the concerns would be conflicting opinions in the clan and an escape being made more difficult. The senior vassals developed the plan and under strict secrecy sent the envoy to Koshu."

They looked dazed and were struck dumb. But their tempers could be cooled. For a short time, a heavy silence charged the dangerous expressions that had been missing from their faces for several seasons, and they exploded.

11
THE NAPPING PILLAR

"**WHY WAS AN** emissary sent from Echigo to Koshu?"

"Is this clan prepared to toss off being a military family? This is humiliating. We will know shame."

"You say we should consider sending an emissary to cling to peace. Well, warriors also get fed up. Moral principles are a waste. The senior retainers who probably hoped for the current situation dulled the lord's determination. This is intolerable. This absolutely cannot be overlooked. We must intrude upon either the residence of Lord Naoe Yamato-no-kami or Lord Kakizaki Izumi to question their motives. All those who agree will come."

"Are you coming?!"

"Yes, we are."

Nearly all of the more than ten men who happened to be present stood and went out to the large corridor. Only one was leaning against a large pillar. His eyes were shut and he didn't stand.

Someone noticed and urged him to come.

"Yataro, aren't you coming? Hurry up."

He raised his sleepy head to show a face dotted with white pockmarks and declared, "Not going."

THIS TIME THIS AUTUMN

"**WHAT?!**"

The group flushed with anger and returned to surround the pillar Yataro was leaning on.

One asked, "You're not going. Does that mean there's no reason to go?"

Yataro answered precisely, "Yes."

"It's better if you don't make this pointless fuss. A child never knows how much his parents love him," he repeated without changing his sitting position.

His attitude and his tone of a warning greatly affected the group's spirit. The man named Demon Kojima Yataro of the Uesugi clan was one of the Ten Tigers of Mount Kasuga, a label heard throughout this land. The Ten Tigers, dubbed that by some unknown person, were elite men selected from hatamoto under the command of Kenshin.

Now, his colleagues did not believe anyone of them compared favorably to Yataro. If an opportunity arose, each one would perform distinguished military service equal to the acts of the others. Even without being one of the Ten Tigers, each had the self-confidence of only seeing success whether glory meant slaying a two-headed or a ten-headed dragon.

"You pockmarked fool!"

Naturally, his arrogance angered his colleagues. He raised one hip to adjust his sitting position and listened to voices from both sides.

"What's the reason for this useless disturbance? It's pointless."

"Aren't you mad an envoy is being sent to ask for peace with Koshu province our long-standing enemy and the double-crosser Shingen?"

"Don't you think it disgraces all of Echigo and Uesugi's army?"

A comrade drew closer and said, "Can you sit and watch? This is not a pointless disturbance. I will give courage and serious reflection to the foolish and calculating senior vassals who lack determination. I'm pressing for a decision. Why is that useless?"

Yataro insisted again, "It's useless," and adjusted his sitting position.

"You're still saying that?"

Some severe-looking members of the group grabbed their long swords and approached him, but Yataro quietly explained to all of them without bothering to look at each man's face, "Calm down and listen. We, the rank and file, had no way of knowing about the deliberations over several days. The senior vassals should not have determined an important war council related to our destiny without consulting us. I have no doubt the policy was conducted before the lord and for the lord. If so, aren't sending an envoy to Koshu and seeking a peace accord the lord's intentions? Is it Lord Kenshin's idea? Are you saying you're displeased with the lord's idea?"

"No, some of the senior vassals surely obscured the lord's ideas, prayed in vain for safety, and complained. Therefore, …"

"You're being ridiculous," said Yataro pushing back at this gossip.

"A samurai gives his life to serve his lord. Where is the lord's spirit in his castle? What is his daily temperament? All of you serve without asking these sorts of questions. You will not give your life. War strategy is not only to pound the *taiko* drums then fight the enemy. The subtlety is the child who doesn't know his father's heart. Instead, the clamor of clumsy rage troubles the lord's mind. In other words, my sort of great patience is only an impediment…. He returned a short time ago from the expedition to Kanto and doesn't look eager to go to the battlefield. Your loyalty may be to relax."

He smiled and in conclusion said, "You see. Of all men, Saito Shimotsuke was chosen and dispatched to Koshu. In spite of the many men to choose from in the clan, Shimotsuke was sent. This judgment was surely not made by the senior vassals. It's the lord's choice. I graciously ask, What is it? or Is it understood? in the lord's heart. Is that too hard to guess?"

No one was angry anymore. The indignant voices and disgraced shouts enveloped not only there but also inside and outside Kasugayama Castle in a rumbling clamor were silenced. The announcement of another campaign and, of course, signs of armaments were not seen. The comings and goings to various supporting castles centered on Kasugayama Castle were sluggish. Fall festivals in the towns and villages were livelier than usual. During times of war, even the blacksmiths and armorers joined in the circles and danced.

13
SHINGEN

WHEN LOOKING ANYWHERE in the sky, the basin valley should have been a mountain. The castle was a small flatlands castle. Its scale was indescribable. This place was also called the Koshu residence or Tsutsujigayaki Yakata. This was the home base of Takeda Shingen in Kofu.

At that time, Shingen was forty-two years old. He had a thick neck and a solid build. His cheeks were full, and the color of his blood radiated like a young man from beneath his dark skin. Whether looking at the palms of his hands or the razor scars on his cheeks and his temples, he was a hairy man.

Judging from his appearance, his unmatched vigorous clan and will of steel were immediately felt. But, as much as possible, he did not display his hard-boiled reasoning. The wrinkles drawn at the corners of his eyes softened his look. He tried his best to maintain the demeanor of an aloof man close to being genial. His eyelids covering large black pupils did not appear to have been dampened by tears.

While leaning his elbow heavily on the armrest, Shingen brought his mouth closer to Atobe Ooi's ear to ask, "Ooi, have you seen the envoy?"

He quietly answered, "No. When the Echigo envoy passes into the envoy room, we'll be notified by a ringing bell in the page's room."

"I still haven't heard a bell."

"When I do, the envoy will not be passed to the next room."

"I want to see this envoy, too."

"You will see him," said Ooi then stood and immediately went to the large papered sliding door already open about two inches to open it a little more.

This place in a corner of the castle was called Bishamondo Temple. Although built to be a temple, it was furnished with Shingen's living room, a library, a council room, and an envoy room. The man Saito Shimotsuke, a vassal of Echigo, who came earlier as a special emissary to this province, will be called here today and seen after a peek at his determined expression. On the one hand, polite courtesy is extended to ambassadors from other provinces, but this sort of impoliteness seems to be common, particularly, when the other side takes on his role with pride in its superiority.

Just like this time, Shingen always enraged Kenshin and imagined he would launch a raid on Usui from Joshu or retaliating on the undermanned Shinshu side.

But nothing happened.

At his leisure, Kenshin began a siege of Odawara Castle, passed through three provinces from Joshu, and withdrew to Mount Kasuga in faraway Echigo.

Shingen witnessed this but saw no obvious signs. The reports coming from the many spies who entered Echigo provided no evidence of troop movements. One thought gave him a bit of relief. Last year, as expected, Kenshin had been exerting himself without a break by going to the front in Etchu, then going to Kyoto for no good reason, and going on an expedition to Soshu that lasted more than six months. Kenshin looked tired. Shingen laughed at the clumsiness of his strategy.

The Echigo vassal Saito Shimotsuke entered Kofu with his deputy Kurokawa Osumi.

Shimotsuke presented Kenshin's letter.

> Lord Kenshin received the words from Lord Shingen with
> genuine interest. I have come to negotiate directly with the
> lord concerning this grave matter and await the day for an
> audience with the lord.

Until that day, the envoy had been waiting in the embassy outside the castle to be summoned.

Kenshin's letter was the same as an envoy's letter but did not touch on the objective. It only referred to the peace reconciliation signed four years earlier with the graciousness of a death poem. After that, with no subterfuge, he asked with extreme courtesy, Was there a reason for the attack on Warigatake Castle while he was away on a campaign? He was not the least bit agitated and voiced no protests. He wrote that he was appealing to the lord's sense of fairness.

It was not Shingen who blushed about this death poem exhausting the facts and sentiments. Several years earlier the two provinces signed a friendship treaty, but have clashed in bloody battles three times at the Shin'etsu border between the Shinano and Echigo provinces. The elite force of Echigo and the mystery of Kenshin were sufficiently understood. Nevertheless, Shingen was unable to erase his contempt for Kenshin somewhere in him. Kenshin was nine years younger than he. When Shingen viewed Kenshin's territory, wealth, and weaponry from any angle, he couldn't control his feelings of contempt and wondered, Who is this man Kenshin?

When he heard an envoy had come, before looking at the letter, intuition told him, He came to mediate for peace.

He believed if Kenshin were inclined to fight, he would have no reason to send an envoy. Being caught off guard would be inevitable.

When he opened Kenshin's letter, he thought, Of course!

Shingen anticipated everything. In any case, he had to listen to the message and respond. However, his vassals told him that the special envoy was a bit strange. What kind of man was he?

His curiosity piqued, before granting the interview, Shingen quietly went with Atobe Ooi to the adjacent room to peek into the envoy room.

14
A CHAIN OF SIGNAL FIRES

FROM THE DAY an envoy arrived from another province, Shingen assumed the roles of host and guide to that guest. Of course, he was also an interrogator and a hospitable guard.

After a stay of several days, today was the day Shingen would meet the envoy. Only Saito Shimotsuke was allowed to pass into the envoy room in Bishamondo Temple. His guides and hosts were Hajikano Den'emon and Magaribuchi Shozaemon.

The way Shimotsuke looked was considered a disgrace even in his hometown. Moreover, every dignitary in Koshu looked disgusted by the sight of him. They thought, This dishonorable, nothing of a man. Not only that, he is a crippled man with one eye and a limp. Never before had they welcomed this sort of envoy from any province anywhere.

"I heard your country of Echigo is a small country of mostly sea but is it a larger country?"

When the host Magaribuchi asked this question, Saito Shimotsuke was not timid and said, "It's as you say, my country is small and only covered by the sea. I heard that Koshu is a mighty power without peer. About how big is it?"

"The length of the country is called the North-South, Eight-Day Road. As proof of this country's expanse, the daily traffic on the highway is said to be one thousand packhorses. Can you guess now?"

"Ha, ha, ha, ha. That is a surprise."

"Why are you laughing?"

"Well, traffic of one thousand packhorses and your pride. In Echigo, boats come and go, one thousand every day. One boat is loaded with the packs carried by one thousand horses. Koshu seems to be an unexpectedly small country."

Magaribuchi turned red and was silent. Trying to rescue him, Hashikano Den'emon said, "Lord Shimotsuke. You're hearing about nonsense. Who in

Echigo deliberately chose a diminutive man like you to send as the envoy to another province? Excuse me for asking, but how tall are you?"

Without making the slightest motion, Shimotsuke answered with no hesitation, "In Echigo, when an envoy goes to another province, for example, if the destination is a powerful province, a large man is sent. And if the province is weak, a small man is dispatched. That is why a small man like me was sent to your province."

Den'emon closed his mouth and said no more. Shimotsuke looking like he was about to burst said, "You asked about my height, but as you see, I'm not that short, just a few inches shy of five feet. You two seem to be five feet, six inches. How many feet do you have on me? Forgive me for saying after just meeting you two, but will you be able to serve as I have your entire lives. Although my sword is shorter than three feet, it will defeat a clothes-drying pole. This irrelevant man was dressed in fine clothes by his lord for this business."

Shingen unwittingly laughed from behind the papered door. However, it was not from meanness. As he roared with laughter, he ordered, "Ooi, open the partition."

Shingen quickly began to speak frankly, "Are you the envoy of Lord Uesugi? You are Saito Shimotsuke? You are quite funny. Long ago, Jun'ukon was ordered by Emperor Sei to go as an envoy to the country of Sou. Along the way, however, he cooked and ate the goose to be given to Emperor Sou and in the audience with Emperor Sou presented him with an empty basket and a paradoxical reason that delighted the emperor. Emperor Sei was said to be amused and praised the honest vassal. You are like Jun'ukon. What is your stipend in the Uesugi clan?"

From a distance, Shimotsuke stepped back and bowed, he respectfully answered, "It is six hundred *kan*."

Shingen listened and muttered, "That's not excessive. Lord Uesugi seems to be generous to his followers."

Then he bluntly asked, "What happened to your eye? Where was your leg crippled?"

Shimotsuke answered with wit and pride in himself but was smart enough to not make the other man uncomfortable.

"If a man is short, he's an influential man, a man sent as an envoy to our clan. Kamakura Gongoro Kagemasa, an ancestor of Lord Uesugi, was robbed of an eye by an arrow of Torimi Yasaburo and gained military fame. Perhaps, you are like that man. Ha, ha, ha. Ooi. Ooi."

"Yessir."

"Give sake to the envoy in great appreciation for his service."

"Yessir."

Shimotsuke interrupted, "Before I take the sake, I have a question."

"What is it?"

"The castle in Warigatake."

"… Oh."

For the first time, Shingen's eyes gleamed. The small wrinkles at the corners of his eyes leaped up. Shimotsuke continued, "Perhaps, the attack was not ordered by the lord, but the Koshu officers and soldiers at the destination committed that violence without permission. In fact, there is deep regret for the name of the rival Takeda clan that pledged close ties of friendship with my Uesugi clan."

"No, the attack on Warigatake was on my order. It was not another man's decision."

"Oh. Why did you give such a command? During Eiroku year 1, the two clans signed an agreement to not go to war and exchanged written pledges before the gods."

"Warigatake Castle was once the territory of the Takeda clan."

"That is not a reason."

"Envoy!"

"Yes!"

"Are you going to drink or not?"

"I will drink after I hear your answer."

"I've given my answer. The bow in your pouch, if you take it out, you can take it out at any time. Will you take sake or take out the bow? What did Lord Kenshin command?"

"From the beginning, to send me here …"

"All right. Well then, drink. Would you like both clans to lock up the oath from the first year of Eiroku?"

"That is unreasonable. I'm only waiting for your answer and then will be able to return as an envoy."

"No, no, you're not the least bit disgraced by your lord's order. Shall I praise you?"

"Not at all. I don't want praise from the leader of Koshu. Today, my first honor is this audience with you. Whether it's tomorrow, the day after, or ten or fifteen days from now, I will wait for your intentions and ask again. I am asking again, please."

"Please? Why are you asking?"

"For proof of a clear apology."

"Ha, ha, ha. That's probably futile."

"It may be futile."

"The sake has been brought out. Will you drink?"

"Yes, now I will. To your health."

Shimotsuke took a large cup. His heavy drinking was in full display to the lord and vassals of the enemy country. However, it was no more than a mild surprise. That evening, an urgent report arriving at Tsutsujigasaki gave a jolt to everyone in the castle. The news was delivered in an instant by a series of signal fires from the Shin'etsu border. A chain of signal fires consists of signal flare pipes provided every two and a half to five miles to sequentially move roaring flames to the main castle in Kofu.

They were constructed to issue an alarm immediately after the cry, "The enemy's attacking!"

Saito Shimotsuke and his party of envoys drove their horses to breakneck speeds by furiously lashing their whips until they were far outside the province.

15

A SHOT OF LIGHTNING

UPON HEARING ABOUT the enemy invasion of Shinano, the blood echoed; the flesh ached; the warriors' excitement could not be contained. This was normal for Uesugi's people in Echigo.

It was a rival country not lacking as a rival. This hostile country had accumulated many grudges. While tying the cords of their helmets and armor, everyone vowed, "We will end it this time," and everyone thought, I must see the head of Tokueiken Shingen.

That was the consistent spirit of ordinary samurai from the commanding officers down to the foot soldiers. In the fights between two provinces for successive years during the Tenbun (1532-1555) and Kouji (1555-1558) eras, every deep-seated grudge from fathers being struck, sons dying, and brothers being lost was diminished. Government policy was Kenshin's creed of holding back Takeda will make the expansion of this province difficult, and the province will have no life. This creed bit deep into the marrow of the entire clan and became their belief like a ball of fire.

Not to mention, the army was out on a campaign this time. They waited and waited.

For forty or fifty days, they only stamped their feet in frustration. Finally, on the fourteenth day of August, Mount Kasuga made lightning strike. The military order was relayed like a motto, To Shinano, To Shinano.

"Uwhaa …"

Out of nowhere, a tsunami of voices curled around the Echigo castle town. In a break in the lightning, armor was donned, horses were led, munitions were gathered, and horses rounded up into a herd. When the army was advanced by the sounding of conch shells and the pounding of taiko drums, the old and young and men and women in the territory suppressed their always tearful voices. The wives of the departing men, the elderly fathers, the sisters, the mothers, and the friends ... were mixed among the force of thirteen thousand.

16
KAIZU CASTLE

IN SHORT, THE thirteen thousand warriors crossed mountains, wandered through valleys, climbed to summits, and cooked meals in villages to swoop down on Shinano from Echigo. The sight was magnificent but the path ahead arduous.

Moreover, everyone vowed not to return home alive along that punishing path.

On the march, roving patrols and important lookouts were provided in four stages before the advance guard. The gun unit, archery unit, spear unit, and warrior unit made up the central force. The unit of packhorses loaded with provisions and soaked in sweat followed last.

"Split into two groups," ordered General Kenshin when they faced the Tomikura-toge mountain pass.

Kenshin was swarmed by the so-called resourceful and brave generals: Nagao Totou-no-kami, Nakajo Echizen-no-kami, Kakizaki Izumi-no-kami, Amakasu Oumi-no-kami, Usami Suruga-no-kami, Wada Kihei, Ishikawa Bingo, Murakami Saemonnojo Yoshikiyo, Mouri Kazusanosuke, Demon Kojima Yataro, Abe Kamon, Naoe Yamato-no-kami, Ayukawa Settsu-no-kami, Takanashi Masayori, and the older and younger brothers Shibata Naganori-no-kami and Inaba-no-kami Harunaga.

"Who? Who goes where? …"

Kenshin called out names one by one to divide the commanding officers and split the force in two. Then he announced, "One force will cross Lake Nojiri and emerge at Zenkoji Temple. I will lead the other force and cross Tomikura and come out near the Chikuma River."

He ordered, "The rendezvous point from whichever direction will not be far from the flow of Chikuma and near Kawanakajima. My force will arrive by the evening of the sixteenth. The other force shouldn't arrive any later than that."

It was already the afternoon of the fifteenth since the army split up. To reach the area of the Sai and Chikuma rivers by the evening of the following day, the armies probably had to march without rest or sleep.

Not one man grumbled in complaint. The ordeal of the marching army was about to start. They suffered for the first couple of days and felt that somehow another body of iron was made apart from himself. In particular, the masses of Echigo did not differ in the least from a fast advancing force because, as a rule, fighting always broke out at the border.

While the sun was still high on the following day, the force commanded by Kenshin passed through Takai-gun and snaked to the Tojo region from the Sorobeku mountain pass.

Kaizu Castle seated entirely in enemy territory was under the control of Shingen's forces, specifically, the elite forces of Kousaka Danjo Masanobu, a general of the Koshu forces famous for his bravery.

"How shall we pursue them?" asked Kenshin as he planned his movements. The shadows of two or three warriors resembling beans on Kaizu Castle's watchtower shaded their eyes with their hands to better see him.

The forces were split up along the way, and Kenshin deliberately took a detour. Until he occupied the base chosen to gain an advantage, he would move to the side away from the castle. His fear was his force would be unable to take up satisfactory positions, and his objectives were control and a show of force.

The castle commander Kousaka Danjo was, no doubt, always among the small human figures that climbed up the watchtower beside the castle.

"They've come," he said while looking but remained calm. Locations outside of Kofu had already been notified by a chain of signal fires. He seemed to want to move cautiously.

"Let's see ... How far will they advance?"

As if unsure, the men in the castle shaded their hands and stared at the destination of the Echigo army.

The flags led by Kenshin crossed two rivers, the Sai and the Chikuma, and set up base on Mount Saijo about two and a half miles south of the castle. When visible, another force flowed in the pitch black from Zenkoji Temple to meet in the same location and finally gained a foothold. The packhorses corps at the rear lowered the loads on the backs of the horses and the ox carts. Around the time the bright red sun set, each company had arrived and was positioned in the vicinity of Mount Saijo. The flags frequently called to the wind, and the warhorses neighed.

"Those are odd places.... Those positions aren't right. They are too far deep into hostile territory."

According to the military science known by Kousaka Danjo, this formation was inexplicable. He could not fathom the enemy's intentions, but he hardened the castle and was determined to wait for Shingen's arrival.

17
THE FIRST GEESE SIGHTING
OF THE NEW YEAR

THE EVENING OF August 16 in the Zenkojidaira basin hugging the Sai and Chikuma rivers swept away the lingering heat of the summer day. The breeze cooled the starry night. After night fell, the vast sky sustained a dim brightness.

Kenshin's troop headquarters were located at the center of the encampment.

The soldiers were cooking their meals and feeding the horses.

"Tonight sleep to your heart's content," Kenshin told the generals to his left and right and gave the same order to his own body.

However, his thoughtful generals, who also acted as close advisers inside the curtains of the field headquarters, looked apprehensive. Tension like a sudden onset of sleeplessness would not be easily erased from their faces.

Wasn't the enemy castle at Kaizu right before their eyes?

Moreover, the position on Mount Saijo invaded too deep into enemy territory.

Kousaka Danjo had rallied the people of Shinano allied with Shingen. At the same time, launching an attack on the castle gates would not be easy.

Not to mention, there were also the fatigue they've carried for a long time and the threat of a surprise attack.

Anyone would think so. Those ideas were common sense. And common sense would lead to the conclusion that the people were secretly terrified.

"Only this time, we cannot understand the lord's tactics. This indiscretion is unusual. This matter is uncertain."

But Kenshin ignored the danger of his position because Kaizu Castle was right there. After Kenshin finished eating the same crude food provisions as the soldiers and slurping up the soba noodles boiled in a bowl of hot water,

37

he ordered Nakajo Echizen-no-kami, "Go listen to the scouting reports. At midnight, the night is cold so keep the bonfires burning bright. The soldiers and their replacements should warm themselves to get ample sleep."

Kenshin immediately turned the war curtains dampened by the evening mist into his walls, some shields into his floor, and flopped down onto his side. Accustomed to sleeping in this sort of simple life, he napped with the dew with grass as his pillow. Once in a while he composed a poem or hummed a song.

During the Noto campaign, he created a work for far in the future.

> A camp covered in frost.
> Fresh autumn air.
> Several lines of wild geese fly over.
> The moon of the thirteenth night shines bright.

He imagined a poem for a young man.

> One armored sleeve of the soldier is laid down,
> And he sleeps.
> From his pillow he hears
> Vivid cries of the first geese of the year.

18
THE HEAVY CURTAINS
OF THE FIELD HEADQUARTERS

NAOE YAMATO-NO-KAMI, THE Magistrate of Packhorses, camped at the gateway to the base. To prevent being caught off guard, he did not sleep alone but with a subordinate, and slept facing the bonfire as he sat on a camp stool.

The reports of a gun echoed. It was nearby.

His eyes opened in confusion. The flames of the bonfire burned in Yamato-no-kami's pupils as he listened to the echoes.

"What direction did they come from?" he asked as he emerged from the war curtains. A lone sentry answered, "I think from Tadagoe."

That was between them and Kaizu Castle. Perhaps he was the patrol of an ally or an enemy patrol taking exploratory shots. As a precaution, Yamato ordered a soldier to run and ask the allied advance guard in the vicinity of Omura if the direction changed between shots and waited for the reply.

Similarly enveloped by fear, both Kakizaki Izumi-no-kami and Shibata Naganori-no-kami stationed on Mount Saijo came down. They asked, "Is Lord Naoe in?"

When they got close, Yamato-no-kami nodded. In quiet, apprehensive voices, the two asked, "Are you having trouble sleeping, too?"

"All the commanding officers in the entire army probably share the same thoughts tonight and are jittery. We are projecting deep into enemy territory and based on a mountain equal to a remote outpost between the two great rivers of Chikuma and Sai. What will we do if a battle breaks out? I can't fathom what's in the lord's heart.... Isn't a place like this usually called a deathtrap in military strategy?"

"What will the lord do?"

"I suspect he will get a good night's rest."

39

"Preferably, everyone should try to look into his own heart. It does no good to fear one's will because only panic sets in."

They went to see Kaji Aki-no-kami who agreed with them.

When Nagao Totou-no-kami and his force arrived, he alone repeatedly stressed the unfortunate layout of the land.

In time, seven or eight agreed with him. Late in the night, a hatamoto said to a page, "I'd like to have an audience with the lord," and sent him as an intermediary to Kenshin.

It was bright inside the field headquarters. Wood had probably been added to the bonfire. Kenshin immediately stood and asked, "What is it? Everyone seems to be here," as he scanned the group. They all looked like they hadn't slept and were looking to find fault.

Nagao Totou-no-kami interrupted to explain the group's concerns. He timidly offered their opinion.

"If Shingen of Koshu comes with a large force, this base will put us at a disadvantage. Our advice is to find a better location now and move the camp at any cost. We also believe you have a secret plan ..."

Kenshin laughed and said, "So that's it?"

"Every last commanding officer is worn out and should be resting tonight. We believe a discussion, even if it's tomorrow, will wipe away all of our anxiety. So we came right away to confide in you.... Everyone is not here yet. The missing Murakami Yoshikiyo, Takanashi Masayori, and Nakajo Echizen-no-kami, should be summoned immediately. Then, perhaps, Kenshin, you will reveal everything."

As they waited, firewood was added to the bonfire.

19

AN ARMY IN A DEATHTRAP

THE GENERALS WERE crammed inside the war curtains. Their fully armored knees were linked in a large circle.

When Kenshin saw the group had assembled, he quietly began to speak.

"Each one of you has predicted this mountain will become a deathtrap and is concerned about my positioning the force here. In no way is this place safe. It's reasonable to call it a deathtrap."

The tone of his voice rose when he said, "Think about it. I will not enter the deathtrap but will somehow control the enemy's death. Not to mention, our rival is the famous Shingen who is resourceful and experienced. The drive to the front this time is a chance to get closer to the old tiger Shingen. Will he be killed? Will I be killed? Victory or defeat will be decided in one fell swoop. When I go to war, I secretly make a vow to the god of war on Mount Kasuga."

When going to war in a battle at any time, the serving of the god of war in the castle on Mount Kasuga and the holding of the *Butai* ceremony have been customs of the Uesuga clan. At that moment, the commanding officers redrew the figure of Kenshin one more time in their eyes.

"As everyone knows, the belligerent posture of Shingen usually is to assemble a force, sneak deep inside waving his flags, and take the chance to turn or move quickly. He's a general who is not easily moved, thoughtful and far-sighted, and not inclined to lightly use soldiers. Although already seen several times since the Tenbun era among weapons of war, his core was not easily crushed. The strangeness of his tactics and his ingenuity were uncommon.

"Closing in on the enemy in one stroke for an unrivaled battle is difficult through a mediocre strategy. Instead, the only tactic was devised by him. Because I am young, this time my actions will probably be reckless and anxious, but have no doubt, I will not be rash or eager. How will Shingen solve this problem of an army of warriors who dare to enter, even under the gaze of the world, a critical land where death is narrowly escaped? We will demonstrate the idea of Zen to him. The actions arising from selflessness in Zen solved by him, the actions arising from selflessness in Zen believed by us, and the resulting changes and actions are difficult to speak of. Right now, they are only seen in our military tactics."

Kenshin stopped talking, closed his eyes for a short time, then spoke aloud again and smiled, "In the open hostilities this time, he is unjustified, and we are righteous. I have earnestly waited for this day. Starting with you, doesn't the entire force resent my smooth rise? At this point, no one should be asking from his heart about positioning the base camp for safety. Only certain victory is expected. This expectation of certain victory is natural. If we are seen, won't this camp that appears to be at a disadvantage and reckless, and the mountain of great patience and adaptability be seen in a glance? ... Ha, ha, ha, ha. First, get a good night's sleep, and we will take a broader view one more time come daybreak. The width of the Sai River, the length of the Chikuma River, and this place are enemy territory. The view here is always favorable. I intend to wake early. If everyone is satisfied, return to camp one by one and sleep.... What is happening tonight at Kaizu Castle? And will there be movement all day tomorrow? Will they reveal themselves?"

The calls of geese threaded often through the clouds.

20
ESCAPE FROM THE ENEMY'S REALM

THE CONNECTED SIGNAL fires delivered shocking news. The province, particularly in Kofu at the center of the provincial government, was in chaos from top to bottom. That was dead midnight on the night of the fifteenth.

One, two, as many as eight warriors came on horseback.

The samurai turned at the crossroads then again at another crossing and headed at full speed with great vigor toward the gate of Ryuuou Road.

Normally, they would have quickly caught the attention of people wondering, What's going on? But the place had been in an uproar since the evening. Are they off to war? Was there an urgent message calling them to join allies in various regions or a demand to join a battle? No one was surprised. No, there was the air of no time left to wonder.

"Retreat! Go back!"

"Open the gate!"

"Step to the side of the gate!"

The shrieks sounded like they were raiding the enemy. They were the cries of warriors. During the night, about ten warriors on horseback kicked up a white cloud of sand, formed a unit, and slammed into the gate at the road portal. This was the gate barrier of the town that was rarely passed through. The horseman in front shouted, "Emergency! We're going through without permission." He jumped off his horse, removed the bar, and quickly pushed open the gate.

"Go! Go!"

He jumped back on his saddle and galloped through like a bullet.

Naturally, the officer and soldiers on guard shouted, "Wait!" and didn't neglect to demand, "Who the hell are you?"

But one after another, the warriors on horseback burst through the barrier gate roared, "This is on the lord's order. The lord's business."

He loudly called out his name and added as he passed through, "I'm the vassal Hajikano Den'emon ... I'll give you the details on the way back. A report is not needed."

Since it was an emergency that night, the guards managed to adapt.

"What? Under the lord's order, the vassal Hajikano Den'emon went through on an emergency?"

He watched the faint white dust kicked up in the darkness.

The sounds of the horse's hooves were heard again from the town. Their ears were buffeted by echoes of armor clustered together galloping closer. In no time, they saw a force of about one hundred men armed with a mixture of long-handled swords, long bare swords, white spearheads, bows, and iron guns.

"Gatekeepers. Gatekeepers. The envoy Saito Shimotsuke from the enemy province, Kurokawa Osumi, and others escaped the embassy in the castle town. They probably won't pass through here, but if they do, arrest them. Arm yourselves and harden this position," shouted the arriving commanding officer at the lead to the guardhouse as he quickly tied the reins while calming his restive horse.

21
ZEN IN THE MOUNTAINS

"**LORD SHIMOTSUKE, THAT** went well," said Kurokawa Osumi who went out a little ahead. Saito Shimotsuke slowing down his horse came next and turned to look in the other directions.

The road was pitch black where they stopped. Mountains soared like a wall before them. From the sounds of water, they guessed only mountain streams flowed nearby.

"I'm not so sure," replied Shimotsuke.

They didn't look at each other. Although twinkling stars were high in the sky, the darkness was so thick the stars' brightness did not pass through.

"Did we lose anyone?" asked the same voice.

The deputy envoy Kurokawa Osumi said to the attendants, "Everyone, call out your name. Say your name."

The ten men who left Echigo beginning with the senior envoy Saito Shimotsuke followed by the deputy envoy on down to the petty servants formed a line.

"We are here. All ten. No one is missing," someone finally answered.

"All right," said Shimotsuke nodding in relief. He fell silent for a short time then dismounted.

"Ahead are only the mountains of Amagoi, Kurakake, and Houraigatake. To avoid them, the foot of Yatsugatake straight ahead is the fastest path. But Shingen opened a road called Boumichi as his military supply route for frequent trips to the borders. Of course, fences and fortresses have been built at various locations and passing through would be impossible," explained Shimotsuke who knew the geography of the enemy country as if it were his garden at home.

Then he said, "In the end, there's no way other than to cross the mountains by foot where no paths exist and fall where one can only fall. Each one of you will abandon his horse and walk. We will cross this mountain

45

stream and enter these mountains."

The feelings of despair were natural and everyone was silent. They left their horses without a word. Shimotsuke ordered the lowest-ranking attendant to gather the ten horses and securely hitch them in the nearby forest.

"What will we do about the enemy's horses? We'll just leave them. They'll be fine."

Some men were anxious to go, but Saito Shimotsuke nodded and said, "If we use the farmers' packhorses, they know their stables and return alone from the fields. If these domesticated horses are free, they'll immediately fly back home along the original trail. In that case, they will become the guides for our pursuers."

However, his wisdom and thorough preparation would not turn out that way. Soldiers under the command of Hajikano Den'emon already knew about the blunder of the men protecting the gate outside the castle and the getaway of Saito Shimotsuke's party through there. Soldiers under the command of Magaribuchi Shozaemon soon swooped down on this mountainous terrain and were closing in on the mountain.

Furthermore, a warrior on horseback immediately flew toward Shingen's Boumichi Road with orders to contact the strongholds ahead. Finally, at dawn, Saito Shimotsuke's unit was trapped on Mount Amari.

By seeing the swiftness of their movement and the skill in communication, they understood the thoroughness of Shingen's supervision compared to the norm. Saito Shimotsuke was well aware of that and instantly realized the stupidity of trying to escape.

"We're trapped."

In the forest on Mount Amari, he said to the others sitting nearby, "It's useless. There's no escape. It's good to clear one's mind before making a decision. Isn't it good to view the autumn scene at daybreak?"

"…"

Their eyes were bloodshot and their grievous lips were set as they strained to hear any sound and searched for an escape route in Shimotsuke's words.

"The enemy is waiting. Will it be a sword fight to the death?"

At last, they seemed to have made up their minds and followed Shimotsuke. Wherever they were standing, they sat down on the fallen leaves.

Autumn was already deep in Kai. Frost covered the bright red and yellow leaves on the trees behind them. The light at dawn reflected down to the bottom of the valley and created fine rainbows within the morning frost. And birds peppered the air with songs in high-pitched chirps.

22
THIS LIFE

"..."
"..."

Everyone yielded. They waited for their pursuers and looked determined to die in sword fights.

The sounds of birds washed over their ears. Their eyes looked at autumn covering the mountain and seemed to desire something from far away.

It was autumn back home in Echigo.

Each of their homes was there. They prepared their minds in advance for this mission into enemy territory. The time had come, and they did not flounder.

But ...

They saw signs of the enemy approaching thick and fast from the valley, from the back and from the front, and leaped up and grabbed hold of their long swords.

"They're coming ..."

"There's no time left to think."

"Needless to say ..."

In the confusion, all eyes brightened. A dreary spirit rapidly arranged on their brows and their lips. Their bodies stiffened like hedgehogs.

"What is death by a sword? That alone is stupid. They can't take away our attack in any fight. Attack! Attack!"

Saito Shimotsuke rubbed his bad left eye in the glare. Given the hardships of the last dozen or so days and the last night with no sleep, his eye was made bleary by sleep.

All eyes faced forward.

"Well,... Do you have the heart for *seppuku*?"

Kurokawa Osumi and the others encircled and closed in on him.

"No, it's not that. Don't misunderstand me."

47

He wiped the sleep from his eyes and was relaxed.

"There will be no seppuku.... What have you planned?"

"We will be captured. If we do this, we'll be arrested. We will be hauled off to the place where prisoners are taken."

"Then what?"

"We'll just live a little longer. Loyalty. I think that is loyalty."

All of them looked stunned. No one expected to hear such cowardly words from Shimotsuke. Especially, the deputy envoy Kurokawa Osumi spoke like he was spitting only at the brave man, "What is loyalty? To become a prisoner of war is to live in shame. Lord Shimotsuke, those words are beneath you. Is something wrong?"

"No, not at all. Escape was impossible from the start. When it's not possible, accept being captured and tied up. Being prepared was decided second. That is natural. It's loyalty."

"But why?"

"Being captured on the battlefield is a different problem. But the mission assigned to me this time was not to fight. The lord's will was for me to come as an envoy to negotiate peace. I was ordered to come and work toward finding a compromise. What purpose does this party of envoys serve if we are killed?"

"It's a reason. It's a reason because you want to live."

"I want to live. I want to live longer. That is the truth. Surprisingly, I have summoned my courage. The circumstances of wanting to live are not the problem of the ego. What is the fate of our still young lord or the future of our country of Echigo? When I thought about all the difficulties and struggles ahead, I grieve over this short life. If the province of Kai were our only enemy, it would not be enough to fear. The lord's talents will never be conquered and controlled by Shingen Harunobu.... But you don't know about a greater desire in the heart of our lord Uesugi Kenshin."

"..."

"Kurokawa, your ancestors and mine descended from the Nitta clan and Wakiya Yoshisuke. This blood still pulses in us and has not disappeared since the time of Nitta Yoshisada.... In the Uesugi clan, that spirit has been carried beginning with the lord, forms the rules of the warrior, and has become the great ambition of a samurai. A vow is made before the god of war each time a warrior goes to war. You certainly already knew that."

"No, the name of the Echigo Warrior will be dishonored."

"Almost nothing will happen if I live, but if I die, they will laugh. Praise and blame are not considered during that time. My mission as an envoy was fulfilled. If I'm captured alive, there is no shame.... You will all do as I do."

They were already surrounded in the forest by the armored Koshu soldiers. Their presence was surmised from the brilliant glinting of the spears, long swords, and armor in the gaps between the trees.

23
THE STRAW SANDALS OF OXEN

THE HIGH-RANKING BUDDHIST priest in his scarlet vestment faced the altar and kindled a holy fire of burning cedar sticks. The body of Shingen in full armor below appeared to be curled at his shoulders and hip.

The large gathering of devoted priests and generals under Shingen's command sat in a row enveloped by the smoke of the holy fire filling the temple. The ringing from time to time of bells cursing the enemy country and the voices chanting sutras could be heard as far as Unpouji Temple at the foot of Mount Sakeishi.

A long time passed. On the seventeenth day, the afternoon sun was beginning to set far beyond Fuefuki River.

A custom of military commanders before going to battle was to purify the mind and body in some way. Uesugi Kenshin followed Shinto ceremonies to worship the gods. Takeda Shingen's custom was to begin by praying at Unpouji Temple on Mount Sakeishi.

Starting the previous evening, Shingen immediately left the Koshu residence Tsutsujigasaki Castle and waited to pray for victory in battle and to practice Zen meditation with allies who joined him at the temple.

Given his influence, once he summoned them in a written declaration, how many troops would gather?

When looking from Mount Sakeishi, a glance took in some uncountable number of troops.

Needless to say, they were inside the temple compound grounds, on the mountain, and in the gardens of the sub-temples. Flags and banners, and the neighing of horses faded into the far-off road at the base of the mountain, people's homes, and the countryside. The view seemed to flicker like there was movement and no movement in the autumn afternoon sun. The warriors as well as the horses were filled with a fighting spirit and could be seen waiting for the order to advance.

While this was happening, the ten including Saito Shimotsuke in the envoy party were roped together like the beads of a rosary and being hauled off. Of course, they were defiant.

"That one?"

"That one."

"I'll kill you."

"From the beginning, there was going to be a blood offering on the mountain."

"You're shamelessly dragged here and won't bite your tongue. Cowards!"

The road was blocked. Before them, soldiers of Koshu and common people shouted abuse at them. This envoy was eloquent and tricked the minds of his allies into compromise. Echigo's power had been thrust among them and already occupied strategic positions. This rumor reached the ears of the rank and file and heightened their indignation.

The carefree look on the face of Shimotsuke like his bad eye was unable to see the mood among the enemy by using only half of his eyes. The Koshu warriors could only hate that face and threw the straw sandals worn by oxen at him as they shouted.

"One-eyed fool!"

"Gimp!"

However, when they entered the compound on the mountain, many generals and hatamoto adept at strategy were present. Thus, discipline took hold and not the slightest bit of meanness was heard. Instead, an air of dread closed in on their bodies to strangle ten spirits.

24
A MASS OF FLAMES

SHINGEN SAT ON a camp stool in front of the main temple. The scarlet vestment on his armor and his angry face looked like a mass of flames. Ten men were seated at the foot of the stairs. Nine men were in back, and one, Saito Shimotsuke, was pushed out and seated in front.

Shingen glowered with his eyes flaring like torches. This feeling took a long time to extinguish. Shimotsuke looked in silence at Shingen's face.

"Envoy. No, lowlife. One-eyed cripple. Why don't you answer?"

Saito Shimotsuke sounded like he was trying to soothe Shingen's feelings when he said, "Has the lord already forgotten my name? I am Saito Shimotsuke, a vassal of Kenshin."

Shingen abruptly shouted in his innate thunderous voice. His blood color and meaty shoulders appeared to swell like bumps. He was forty-two and different from his younger self, Takeda Harunobu. His discretion came just in time for the moment of rising fury. A grin immediately materialized. The tone of his voice changed when he asked, "Yes, yes, are you the envoy Saito Shimotsuke from Echigo? I will ask again, until yesterday under the pretext of the words of Kenshin, you wanted to solidify peace again for the coming year. Prepared to find a compromise. You were to be courteous, hold your tongue, lower your head, and be attentive to me. That was probably your strategy ordered by Kenshin before you left.... You came as an envoy because you knew or didn't know in your home country that warriors would unexpectedly appear in Shingen's domain. Tell the plain facts. Speak the truth …"

25

GRINNING DEFIANCE

SHINGEN'S QUESTION NOT only had the obvious meanings of the words but concealed his intention to extract something from Saito Shimotsuke's answer.

In addition to ideas on the war strategy he immediately understood out of necessity, the most troubling problem he faced was the extent of the determination of the enemy nation. He probably read that hint from Shimotsuke's expression. The plan of the very shrewd general at that instant was to listen to Shimotsuke.

Shimotsuke may have realized that or wondered what he thought and at that moment burst into laughter.

"Aha, ha, ha. Wha, ha, ha."

He laughed so that his stained front teeth would not jut out. He suppressed his laughter to answer slowly and deliberately.

"It's been said for some time that you, the lord of the Koshu residence, Kizan Daikoji, possesses a fearsome intellect. Your question is snatching away the cake held by a child to soothe him and softens your appearance considerably."

He was dismissive. Not only about Shingen, but also spoke indiscreetly about his top generals around him. Of course, he stirred strong emotions in the brilliant, iron-helmeted generals present. Their unmoving, sharp gazes, trembling bodies, and silence exerted an unseen force on Shimotsuke. However, Shimotsuke did not react. His trait of one bad eye enabled him to maintain an air of calm in this sort of situation. He constantly blinked one eye and spoke again when Shingen finished.

"I don't know about other provinces, but in my Echigo, the army's plan and the domestic administration are all the responsibility of Lord Kenshin. He restricts his consultations to a small number of senior vassals and the field headquarters staff. You can see that I am a rank-and-file soldier.... You are asking whether I came as an envoy knowing that or not knowing? No matter what you're asking, I am an envoy who was kept in the dark....

"Suppose Lord Kenshin's heart held a strategy that differed from the envoy's message, if the envoy knew and came out among the enemy, he would not be able to fabricate a look of indifference before the lord of the enemy country. The honesty of the man will surface somewhere.

"Everyone in Echigo from Lord Kenshin to the masses understands you as a man who is not inclined to overlook something like that. For example, Lord Kenshin's fatigue can be inferred from his absence in the spring of this year and the Echigo campaigns undertaken year after year. To abruptly break the treaty and seize the border at Warigatake, if you were a cat, these acts would have been impossible to do except for the most sly and cunning of cats."

Again, if a moment later Shimotsuke roared with laughter, the men who influence Shingen or the generals under his command may have immediately applied shoes or spit to his head.

However, Shingen let out the expected forced laugh. To protect himself from an unlikely event, before Shimotsuke's words stopped then didn't, he moved his huge frame and rose from the camp stool. He said, "Place this chatterbox in the custody of the monks at Unpouji Temple until I return in triumph. Tell them to throw him in the cellar. And put all his comrades in jail. I will deal with them when I return."

Shingen's appearance of not having the time to address the fate of these men was instantly reflected in the hearts of his commanders.

Shingen raised his body from the camp stool and turned toward the entire force. He ordered them to depart with "Now!"

The conch-shell trumpeters standing in both corners in the east and west corridor touched the mouths of the shells to their lips and blew loud sounds for long and short intervals. The way of blowing conch shells differed in each province. Nevertheless, the warriors off to war recognized those tones with their entire bodies. In no time, their blood boiled, and their eyes glimpsed visions of the battlefield.

Those sounds told the men left behind throughout the country that the army was on the march. And at that moment, they prayed fervently while tracking the officers and men following the army in their thoughts.

26
BOUMICHI ROAD

A LONG, MEANDERING road extended endlessly to the north. The newness of the road's earthen color revealed its recent opening in the past few years. This road could be said to be a map of Shingen's will drawn on the land. It was a military route of the Kai forces to Shinshu. By traveling this straight road, the province border would be reached a day and a half sooner. Farmers and travelers dubbed this road Shingen's Boumichi, Shingen's pole road.

Boumichi Road was centered on Kofu and branched to the west, east, and south. Therefore, several neighboring provinces of Hojo, Tokugawa, Oda, and Saito had diplomatic relations with Shingen, warred with him, quarreled with him, and made countless visits year in and year out. The feeling was the road was a versatile partner. They pointed at Shingen from the surrounding nations and called him Lord Long Legs of Koshu. His Boumichi Road was said to be for emergencies. From the electric shock this road delivered, hostile provinces might conclude that it was a weakness.

The day the large army stronger than twenty thousand men went there was a thrilling sight. By the morning of August 19, elite warriors and horses moved like a raging current from the base of Mount Yasugatake to Daimon Pass.

Takeda Tenkyu Nobushige on his horse turned to call, "Douki, Douki."

Nobushige was Shingen's younger brother. Under the flags of the 21st Central Army troops, they advanced with the clan of Taro Yoshinobu, the heir of Shingen.

"Did you call me?" asked Yamamoto Kansuke, the sole strategist who entered the priesthood and took the name Douki. A jet-black helmet covered the head of the Buddhist priest, and white eyebrows seemed to grow from between the visor. He was older than sixty.

"What's the weather forecast? ... The weather there looks good. These skies should hold for four or five days."

"Are you asking if it will rain or be sunny?"

Kansuke gulped down the air. His eyes slowly squinted, and he said, "The clouds are fast. Some nights will see rain showers but not heavy rains. During the day the air will not get chilly, and clear skies may continue for several days."

"Until we encounter the enemy, hopefully, the weather will be fair. The men and horses have been worn out by the march."

"Well, we aren't sure where the enemy is. Even if we go there this time, the confrontation between the armies will last a while. As the fighting spirit wears down, a long siege army will be good."

"Why? … Along the way, a warrior came on horseback bringing orders from Shinshu. The enemy Kenshin has crossed both the Sai and Chikuma rivers and advanced deep into allied territory. Naturally, a battle cannot be avoided whether we go there or not."

"That Kenshin mischievously entered deep into our domain for no reason and will continue with these reckless acts. Setting up a base and any unexpected changes are definite concerns."

"If not, conflict is inevitable.… But my guess of his intentions based on sending an envoy like Saito Shimotsuke is that they will ignore us and head out to Shinshu for a sneak attack. He has absolutely no confidence. If he believed in certain victory, he would not send an envoy like that and be playing petty games."

The older brother Shingen brought his horse alongside. He turned his eyes behind the helmet visor to look at his brother's profile and said, "Nobushige, Nobushige, don't speak worthless speculations without reason. Saito Shimotsuke is a fine warrior. He is not ashamed of his lord's orders. Kenshin's skill in using him also reveals an understanding of his enemy enough to provoke him. In any case, my going to war is delayed by one step. If this step is regained, it is clear we will take up arms. As Douki said, his preparations probably seem strange to the enemy. Don't easily dismiss them. Your words carry a subtle effect among the warriors. Taking the enemy lightly even for a moment should not be encouraged in our forces."

Nobushige tamely replied, "Yes," and looked embarrassed to Taro Yoshinobu beside him.

Next, Taro Yoshinobu asked his father Shingen, "When out on a campaign, why didn't the Saito Shimotsuke and other wicked envoys pray for a blood offering? Yesterday, I was sure that would be the outcome."

Shingen's eyes took on the severe expression of a father when he looked again at Taro Yoshinobu.

"The enemy's expectation is hard to avoid. Of course, they will abandon dying for a cause. The group placed no value at dying for a cause and deliberately challenged my wrath. That became their aim."

"Why?"

"A blood offering in my army of the entire party of envoys echoes in despair, but when they hear about it, the blood of the Echigo force will boil and add to their power."

"But for one or two months, there's no reason to transmit that fact to the enemy."

"The report of their arrival said there were twelve envoys in the group. If the number captured on the battlefield yesterday is understood, it was only ten. Two slipped through the net and returned to report to Kenshin. And several tens of Koshu spies will be captured in Echigo.... There's no value in killing them all. No thoughtful general would devise the poor plan of killing the enemy in a blood sacrifice to raise morale. Of course, that was a very likely act when relations broke off with foreign countries such as during the invasion of the Mongols. Hojo Tokimune, the regent of the shogun, was said to have killed his original envoy and a rude envoy of Koma Kudara who had come a long way...."

Before them, a vast cloud of dust approached.

The banner insignia instantly identified the army. They were not the enemy but allies joining en route.

This was a chance meeting with the three hundred warriors of Koshiba Keishun and Kurita Eijuken who controlled the area near Zenkoji Temple.

They were called The Greeters and preceded two hundred warriors and five hundred warriors in line to join Takeda's party. Therefore, the number of banners of the entire force would increase as the force advanced. The troop strength visibly swelled with each passing mile.

27
A GAME OF BATTLEFIELD POSITIONS

THEY CAMPED FOR several nights.

The Koshu forces crossed Daimon Pass to Nagakubo from Chiisagata.

With the waters of the Chikuma River always in sight, messengers on horseback came in quick succession from the ally's Kaizu Castle to bring news of enemy movements.

"… Uh-huh. Umm."

That's all Shingen said before going silent. Even after hearing the discussion of the men in the field headquarters and the messengers' reports, he only nodded.

Around the time they passed the left bank of the Chikuma River and reached Shiozaki in Sarashina-gun, the troop strength was markedly greater than at the start in Kofu. The faces of the officers and the men were blasted by the autumn winds on the vast plain and erupted in goose bumps.

Someone muttered, "… It's too damn cold. These winds are blowing in from Echigo."

Shimojo Hyobu of Shimoina and his soldiers came galloping. Looking at the arrival order in the ledger of troops arrivals, the usual allies certainly wondered if the samurai of each village and town had joined the battle.

But the entire fighting morale seemed to chill at places. The samurai general Oyamada Yasaburo Nobushige asked with a touch of suspicion, "After coming here, it's odd that the lord now takes these matters under careful consideration. Why only this time a startling order has not yet been issued?"

Nobushige was troubled by other suspicions. The departure from Kofu faced this expansive valley while battling time. Like he was deliberately wasting time, Shingen followed the Sai River, gauged the fast currents of the Chikuma, set up a base on the mountain, guarded the hills, rested the men and horses, and appeared to have not easily settled on a camp location.

57

On the twenty-fourth, Shingen finally appeared to have chosen the location for the troop headquarters when he said, "Here."

The location was a part of Sarashina-gun and a hill of Nobusato. It was called the high ground by the peasants who worked the land around Mount Chausa.

In two lines in golden characters on fourteen feet of dark blue cloth of the *Furinkazan* battle standard of the Takeda clan, displayed four phrases from Sun Tzu's *The Art of War*.

> As swift as the wind. As gentle as a forest.
> As fierce as fire. As unshakable as a mountain.

Under the unceasing fluttering of the standard in the autumn winds sat Shingen with quiet eyes. His eyes were clear not cloudy like he was well rested.

"This is beyond understanding ..."

The same muttering escaped his lips many times.

Mount Saijo, the location of Kenshin's base, was visible from that expansive area hugged by the Sai and Chikuma rivers.

It was serene and quiet.

There was no spirit of the sword.

Topologically, however, that force of Mount Saijo was a hard-to-solve puzzle even with Shingen's years of experience and strategic reasoning. He could only see the stance of risking one's life for others. If he kept changing his position, Shingen could not find serenity.

"The jaws of death ... what place compels the desire to die?"

It's said a wise man is drowned by wisdom. Shingen tried to be cautious. Without wisdom, however, his wisdom could not be penetrated.

"Uh, not here. This place is no good for any ally either."

He twisted around on the camp stool.

Looking around at the men making up the force, he was a little lost about who to approach for advice, beginning with his eldest son Taro Yoshinobu, his younger brother Tenkyu Nobushige, his next younger brother Takeda Shoyoken, or from among Nagasaka Chokan, Anayama Izu, Obu Heibu, Yamagata Saburobei, Naito Masatoyo, Hara Hayato, and Yamamoto Kansuke Nyudo Douki.

The fluttering sounds of the battle standards of Amari Saemon-no-jo, Oyamada Bitchu, Baba Nobuharu, Obata Yamashiro-no-kami, Sanada Danjo, Tokusai, Ogasawara Wakasa-no-kami, Morozumi Bungo-no-kami, Ichijo Nobuhide, Aiki Ichibei, and Ashida Shimotsuke-no-kami; the neighing of the horses; the sounds of the soldiers; and the sounds of the autumn winds collected here.

"Clear out the force and retreat. Leave this place and go down to cross at Amenomiya. Take up stations in front of Chikuma River, on the north shore, and at Amenomiya crossing."

Something seemed to pop into his mind, and he blurted out this order without consulting his senior officers and strategists, contrary to his rule of running his orders past them.

Shingen walked around inside the war curtains. As he walked, he often struggled with his wisdom, like a nearly unbeatable master before a game of Go. With his lips drawn tight, he stared at the ground at his feet. Under the direct rays of the autumn sun, many ants entered and exited an ant hole.

28

A YOUNG WOMAN ON ECHIGO ROAD

KAWANAKAJIMA IS AN old name that predates the Eiroku era and means the island between the rivers.

This broad, triangular mud flat was formed in a part of Zenkojidaira and enclosed by the rapid waters of the Sai and Chikuma rivers. It is mentioned in *Kojiki* (*The Record of Ancient Matters*) as Kawanakajima and Yawatabara. But its broader meaning to the local people was the entirety of the dry riverbed and plain crossing Sarashina, Hanishina, Minochi, and Takai. They were called the four districts of Kawanakajima.

A voice from somewhere said, "… No matter which way I look, all I see is the plain with the same autumn flowers and the same river."

A woman on a journey alone overtaken by darkness looked west and east, and wondered, Which way should I go?

The woman wore a lacquered straw hat. She didn't look like a peddler but looked masculine carrying a package on her back, tying her hem to be short, wearing straw sandals, and holding a cane. She appeared to be younger than twenty. Her smooth, white skin immediately brought to mind a maiden from a snowy country. Her manners and features were those of a beautiful woman particular to the women of Echigo.

She heard the sounds of sickles coming from somewhere. She also heard the pleasant sounds of dry grass being mowed. Her round eyes darted toward those sounds.

She could see the backs of several unsaddled horses among the autumn flowers. In the distance, a man finished stacking bundles of cut grass on a horse's back and pulled the horse off. Later, the crew mowing grass gathered the sickles and continued cutting grass toward the dry riverbed.

"Which way should I go to come out at Koshu Road?" the woman's voice unexpectedly asked. The mowers jumped up in surprise. All of them were farmers from nearby villages pressed into service. These so-called military porters cut horse feed and opened the roads to ease transportation.

"Oh, you say Koshu Road.... Where on earth did you come from?" asked one man. The young woman quickly wandered to watch the flows of the unfamiliar rivers of Sai and Chikuma.

"From over there," she said pointing to the far-off hill where Zenkoji Temple stood.

"Well, does Hokkoku Kaido Road come from the north?"

"Uh, yeah," he nodded but looked uncertain.

The military porters corrected her like they were scolding her. Whether she knew it or not before she came here, this belt of land became a battlefield two or three days earlier. On land only seen in a panoramic view during the day, figures holding hoes and travelers were not seen. If anything passed by chance over the plain, it would be a bird's shadow.

"Why's a girl like you all by yourself hanging around this sort of place? Quick, go over there. Well, go along the riverbank over there and keep going south, soon you'll see the roofs of the town. There you can ask questions about going anywhere in Koshu. Hurry up and get there before dark."

When they finished relaying these bits of information, their hands grasped their familiar sickles. They bent over toward the roots of the grass and quickly began to cut the horse feed as planned.

They still had no idea where she came from. Perhaps, she came from the other shore. Bang! Bang! Bang! Five or six gunshots were heard one after another.

"Get down. Keep quiet!"

"..."

They were patient and stayed down. The gunshots stopped. A white evening haze descended on them.

Heads were slowly raised.

"Get out now!"

Only one was wounded and had to be carried out in a sprint. But when they stood, someone about sixty feet in front of their crew had been hit by a bullet. How unfortunate. It was the young woman from Echigo wearing the straw hat who had walked up to these mowers to ask about the road.

29

STRAY WINDS IN THE FOREST
OF THE HEART

THE LACQUERED STRAW hat whose red cord snapped and dropped into spiderwort flowers where it stayed all night long.

However, the scenery transformed overnight in this stretch of grassy plain going southeast about twenty-five miles from the dry riverbed.

Beginning yesterday around noon, the entire force of Takeda Shingen descended Mount Chausa, crossed Fusegomyo and Shinonoimura, and moved to the front of Amenomiya during the night. When surveyed in the morning, the central unit was right in the center. The twelve units were spread across five lines.

No one had to tell Kenshin on Mount Saijo of their presence. Countless banners were lined up and planted. Each unit came to impress the enemy with their battle standard.

They're getting closer! was the thought even on Mount Saijo. The force was spotted when they shaded their eyes from the morning sun shining through the gaps in the morning clouds.

But in no time, Mount Saijo was covered by morning haze in contrast to the pretentious display by the Koshu force. Since the previous night, the encampment was quiet, and even signs of people waking up could not be observed.

Moreover, the distance between the forces there and here was short.

The river was wide in this area, but if the waters of the Chikuma were crossed, the skirt of Mount Saijo was right on the other shore.

As the sun rose high in the sky, the sense of distance between the two armies shrunk. The morning clouds blurred the standard flags of the Koshu force. White clouds obscuring the yellow, green, and autumn leaves on Mount Saijo gradually cleared up. The clouds burned off allowing both sides

62

to watch the movements of the sentries and the shadows of hitched horses on the other side.

On this day, Shingen in his field headquarters sat on his camp stool and meditated all day long with the enemy on Mount Saijo before him.

"...?"

His expression said the question consuming him from the day before remained unsolved. He questioned the heart of the enemy general Kenshin on Mount Saijo, as well as his will, changes in his will, and his conviction.

These questions bothered Shingen. What sort of ingenious strategy is Kenshin devising? Will he be rash, or act in ways unable to distinguish between good and evil, or be daring?

Like a bird trapped by the rice cake used for bird catching, Shingen struggled with his worries. He sat composed on the stool. In fact, since yesterday, he issued several orders to break off a unit from this army to detour to the northeast of the enemy, come out near Yashiro, and cut off the road connecting to Hokkoku Kaido Road. He also showed the power to cut in two the space to his allies in Asahi Castle of Koshiba near Nagano village that had been requested by Uesugi to act as his sole backup castle. Despite trying to push out this position, there was no will to fight. The lack of expression on Mount Saijo was natural and remained today as it was yesterday.

When he promised a fight with bare swords and stood up, Uesugi Kenshin's posture was to not face his opponents but to simply walk up to their sword guards.

Shingen's worry was the man might be an idiot or unskilled in battle. On the battlefield, Kenshin was the man who knew Shingen better than any man inside the curtained field headquarters. At the same time, the man who knew Kenshin's face in detail and more than the men around him was Shingen.

> As swift as the wind. As gentle as a forest.
> As fierce as fire. As unshakable as a mountain.

The characters on the large, eighteen-foot-tall unit banner raised by him to symbolize his honor fluttered above Shingen's head. He often wondered, What is that? or What's he trying to say? But his heart was resolute in not being silent as it is deep in the forest.

30

THE PARASOL

MORNING CAME again.

It was August 28.

The squads of spies of the great commanders Yamagata Saburobei and Hara Hayato returned along the Susohana River in the direction of Nagano and Zenkoji Temple.

One spy reported, "I saw no movements at Asahi Castle."

Shingen grilled him, "Is Koshiba Kunai at Asahi Castle showing signs of leaving the castle?"

Together Hayato and Yamagata said, "There are none."

"It's inconceivable that the soldiers on Mount Saijo and the soldiers at Asahi Castle are there to lure in our forces into attacking both sides. We have nothing to worry about because allies are positioned to cut off those two sides, so transporting food supplies to Mount Saijo appears to be extremely difficult."

A bubble of terror floated for an instant on Shingen's face. When it disappeared, his past few days of doubt left with it. Kenshin's mindset was reflected, to some extent, in Shingen's heart.

"Den'e, Den'e. Is Hajikano Den'emon here?" Shingen's voice carried inside the curtains packed with hatamoto. The man soon stood there.

"I'm here."

Den'emon ran through the hem of the windblown curtain and kneeled before Shingen's camp stool.

"Den'e? You will be my envoy," he said offhandedly.

"Come closer," Shingen commanded with his eyes. Den'emon was agitated by a sudden feeling and slid closer to the stool on his knees.

"You'll go to Mount Saijo."

Behind him, they wondered, What was the order? Den'emon could barely hear his whisper. On Shingen's side, the top generals and the private secretaries all were a distance away.

In a short time, Hajikano Den'emon dressed in fine attire went to the enemy's Mount Saijo to meet with Kenshin to serve as Shingen's envoy.

He changed everything from his battle surcoat down to his loincloth. Only a battlefield envoy avoids clothes smelling of blood and bloody scars. Of course, if given the chance to be in the enemy's headquarters, needless to say, the *tidiness* of death is sufficiently considered.

Four or five of his followers would accompany him.

They probably included sons off to their first battle ordered by some ally. One was a youthful samurai who looked only thirteen or fourteen years old. This youngster carried a long-handled parasol, When Den'emon finally left the camp and went to the shore of the Chikuma River, the youth opened the parasol with a pop and held it above the lord's head.

This parasol was in no way a meaningless accessory.

The river crossing of the military envoy followed international law, and the parasol was opened onboard the boat. Of course, bullets and arrows were not shot at the boat crossing with the open parasol.

The flat-bottomed riverboat that resembled a large field boat carried the young man holding the open parasol, the lord, and the followers. The boat was pushed by a pole from the north shore of the Chikuma River. A red dragonfly frolicked above the soldier cutting the pole through the fast waters with clean thrusts to move the boat forward. The dragonfly landed and flew off the end of the pole time and again.

31
THE TREK UP MOUNT SAIJO

"**AH ... ARE THEY** from the enemy?"

"It looks like a military envoy. It is a military envoy."

A platoon of lookouts stood at one end of Mount Saijo and never took their eyes off the opposite shore. They shaded their eyes to see this curiosity.

Demon Kojima Yataro was the unit leader of seventy warriors stationed in the nearby barracks. When he noisily emerged from somewhere, he held a hand over his pockmarked face and muttered, "Uuh, that's a samurai named Hajikano Den'emon from Koshu. Why is he coming?"

Of course, a squad of about three or four warriors could be seen dashing from the troops to the dry riverbed to confirm his identity.

As the bow of the boat rode the rolling waves to the shore, they wondered, Where will they go? The unit divided into two lines to the left and right and thrust their fence of spears forward.

This was the protocol to wait for a military envoy. The spears bearing the will to fight were splendid. The color of the parasol coming down in the white light was beautiful. And the military envoy possessed a gracious composure.

"I am Hajikano Den'emon, a Koshu vassal. I know the thoughts of Lord Shingen and would like to meet with Lord Kenshin on this short break from the battlefield. I wish to act as an intermediary."

"Please wait here," said one and ran back to the unit leaving him encircled. In time, the commander came and said, "Your wish is being conveyed. This place is out of the way, so come to my camp to rest."

He led Den'emon to his post and offered him a camp stool. In a short time, Shibata Naganori-no-kami and Demon Kojima Yataro came down more as guards than as a welcome party.

"If you wish to see him, please come with us."

"I'm sorry to be such trouble."

Hajikano Den'emon bowed and followed the duo, leaving the unit, the parasol, and the base of the mountain behind. Alone, step by step, they ascended the mountain path under the flags, iron swords, horses, guns, and arrows of Uesugi's power.

Along the way, Demon Kojima Yataro approached Den'emon's side to ask, "Do you recognize me?"

Den'emon's face showed a hint of a smile and said, "Your face is very hard to forget. If nothing else, the pockmarks are a good sign. It's been seven or eight years?"

"No, not seven or eight years. It was when the armies of Koshu and Echigo met here the last time."

"Ten years. Time flies."

Like old friends, they apologized for the years of silence. However, the two old acquaintances were not particularly warm. Remembering made one's blood run cold.

At that time, Kojima Yataro accompanied Kenshin to the capital for an audience and unexpectedly disappeared on the way to Kyoto. Yataro's disappearance happened with the permission of Kenshin, who already embraced ambitions for the future. Whether there was a tacit agreement or not, for at least several years after that, Yataro went around looking at military preparations and castle fortifications. That was his warrior training for later.

He was in Kofu for some time after that. Of course, entering the country was difficult for a man charged with that sort of mission. Fires burned in the fire pots of the gun blacksmiths in the castle town. He got his hands covered in mud like a plasterer, fired the molding metals, built the fire mounds, and helped with the bellows.

The generals of the Takeda clan entering and leaving the Koshu residence sometimes passed before this establishment on horseback or in everyday clothes. Among them were the eyes of Hajikano Den'emon. One time, he ordered the man with a pockmarked face to bring guns from his establishment.

Yataro delivered them. But he only passed the guns to men inside the residence to be taken over the mountains away from Koshu. If he went inside the gate, he realized he would be tied up where he stood.

However, that alone brought out Den'emon's emotions. If Yataro felt he was in danger of arrest, he probably could not escape the blacksmith's house if encircled. Or if chased by a posse of warriors on horseback, Yataro may not have been able to escape outside the province. Nevertheless, he returned without incident to Echigo.

After that came today and today's chance detente. Thus, the two men's smiles were shrouded by the feelings of unspoken recollections and ironic nostalgia.

32
TOSS-THE-HEAD TATEWAKI

WAR, IN THE end, is the highest expression of power versus power among men. Through all time, men's power has not changed from the starting point of action through the natural course of events. Of course, the actions of political policy, strategy, economy, and work are fully exploited as well as the mountains, rivers, and plains of nature. The beams of light in the white blazing sun were made into allies. The advantages given by dark nights and the darkness of daybreak were employed. Everything in existence from the comings and goings of the clouds, from the direction of the wind to the temperature, and cold, hot, damp, and dry weather conditions were mobilized for action and breathed in life. The heart of *Our Army* was the men and only the power of men.

Thus, a nation at war cultivates men.

If each man did not search or improve, the warring states in this era would be unable to survive. They would be squashed in rapid succession and fall to the wayside.

Even in the life of a man with regrets, the world moves forward without looking back or with no time to look back. The life of a man unable to have regrets was not a life.

Above all, around Eiroku year 4 (1561), more than in the later periods of Tensho and Keicho, more and more people were solidly built. They were courageous, and their lives were laid bare.

The people of Echigo and the people of Kofu were evenly matched.

The battle lines of Uesugi's force and Takeda's force in confrontation gathered the power of those people. The training of the ordinary heart and the discipline of the flesh are concentrated here and stand under the just climate of the universe to both forces.

Under cries of "Now!" different objectives and beliefs are risked here and tested here.

Consequently, depending on this collection and each quality forming

68

those forces, the distinction between character and tenacity or weakness will be determined.

Takeda's force at Amenomiya crossing and Uesugi's force on Mount Saijo were separated by the Chikuma River. When observed from their respective viewpoint, neither could be considered to be strong or weak. Both camps have seasoned warriors, generals who are superb strategists, commanding officers, and soldiers who could all be called talented, able men.

If recommended by the words *good vassals are the foundation of a good lord*, greatness may be found in the leaders Shingen and Kenshin.

The great vassals of Echigo and men with fine reputations in the world were Usami, Kakizaki, Naoe, and Amakasu. The famous four vassals of Koshu were Baba, Naito, Obata, and Kousaka.

In the battle in Haranomachi in past years, a solitary horseman advanced vigorously into Uesugi's force and stabbed his spear at twenty-three enemies. Warriors like Hoshina Danjo also known by the name of Danjo the Spear because of his skill with a spear and Sanada Danjo also called Danjo the Demon because of his distinguished military exploits second to none had many followers.

Both Danjo the Spear and Danjo the Demon were brave warriors of Koshu. And in Uesugi's force, a countless number of men were said to be unbeatable in terms of bravery.

Yamamoto Tatewaki who Kenshin viewed as unusual was also called Asura, after the power-seeking deity. In a fight at any time, whenever the retreat gong sounds to pull back the allies, if he was not the last back, he was not returning from inside the enemy. His returning figure was covered in blood from the top of his helmet to the cords of his straw sandals. No matter which great general's head was obtained, he did not return carrying it attached to his hip. Therefore, it was not recorded in the ledger of military exploits.

When people asked, "Is it useless to go to the trouble of carrying out a great military exploit?"

He answered, "Nothing is useless when one distinguishes himself on the battlefield."

Walking around carrying heads for glory and having the number of heads utmost in his mind hampered his next action.

His nickname in Echigo was Toss-the-Head Tatewaki. However, he was not listed in the record of military exploits and for many years remained a commander of about fifty foot soldiers.

His lord Kenshin met with him for that reason, but there was another circumstance.

The older brother of Yamamoto Tatewaki was named Yamamoto Kansuke Nyudo Douki, a general with a mind for strategy in Koshu and widely known in the world.

On closer examination, he had a different father. Kansuke was raised alone and had a younger half-brother from another father. However, the older brother was said to be in the Koshu army. In several subsequent battles between the forces of Koshu and Echigo, Tatewaki's actions did not change in the slightest and were no different than when he battled any other army.

He was ferocious.

Kenshin usually said, "Well, the actions divided among the armies of the brothers should be difficult as the children of men. The day should bring distressing thoughts to the allies."

He finally abandoned his devotion to the tentative peace negotiations between Koshu and Echigo when the year peace was concluded in Eiroku 1 and dispatched an important vassal to Tokugawa Kurando Motoyasu of Mikawa. The envoy Imokawa Heidayu was always added to a courteous letter from Kenshin.

> A beloved vassal is difficult to send to another clan. However,
> due to various experiences, the man himself knows compassion.
> If separated when separation is difficult, I hope for him to be
> looked after for a long time.

The envoy was made to learn his intentions by heart and repeatedly asked about future prospects.

33

33

33
YATARO AND DAILY TRAINING

DEMON KOJIMA YATARO'S surname was Kojima and his given name was simply Yataro Kazutada but later came to be known only as Demon.

He was born in Kaminogo in Echigo Province, the son of a cattleman. When he was fifteen or sixteen, Kenshin coming from somewhere after a hunt saw that strange creature, brought him home, and entrusted him to Usami Suruga-no-kami's unit.

"Train him."

"Is Yataro a demon's child?" often teased the adults. He was powerful, had red hair, and had a face buried by smallpox scars. According to legend, long ago, the demon leader Shuten-douji came from the sea and landed on the upper district of Echigo Province, and that demon was related to Yataro.

However, when he became a man, that name was no longer funny. He became a frightening, heavy drinker. Being snow country, everyone in Echigo drank a lot, but he was accurately described as a bottomless pit of a heavy drinker. His record was three gallons in one night and five gallons in one day. Moreover, he had an air of self-confidence.

In the Echigo clan in which martial arts were polished as were the men, eating and drinking had hard and fast rules. This is understood from one of the articles in the clan's edicts.

- No excessive drinking. For example, others do not view your drinking as dangerous. And the major organs are not harmed.
- Gluttony is the height of shame. Do not indulge in the pleasures of the self. The best example of enjoying the companionship of fellow vassals is moderation. Excess is to be scorned.
- In general, eating and drinking shall be prudent and discrete. If you fall ill, you will be a disgrace on the battlefield during the morning. If your life is lost, that would go against the two paths

71

of loyalty and filial piety. You will become a figure of mockery in the world, a disgrace to the clan, and inferior to having no success on the battlefield.

This is only one article from the rules of the Uesugi clan to ordinary vassals. However, together with the names of high-ranking generals in the field curtains, Kenshin displayed a version of practice in the warrior's way in a scroll called *Daily Ethics in the Fushikian Clan* to the sons of the clan.

- A life's service begins with the day's work.
- Rise early in the morning and cleanse hands with water.
  Of course, pray to the divine ancestors and Buddha.
- Walk one time around one's residence. First, men shall quickly tie up their hair. The preparation of meals must not exceed two dishes.
- In our clan, everyone is considered to be our child. Mercy and benevolence should be like sprinkling sword powder onto a sword.
- In the evening, our beloved children are not put to sleep by our side. The bedding servants are placed in the warmth, and our children are placed in the cold.

These directives taught Kenshin's attitude regarding the particulars about the daily food, clothing, and shelter to public office, companionship, correspondence, and recreation in morals and training especially of the warriors.

- In addition to one's trade, if one has spare time, one should endeavor to learn.
- Poetry becomes the work of nobles. Warriors may have a little consideration, which is superior to having none.
- A loyal vassal is steadfast, like the wind and the grasses and trees, in protecting the lord's words and the vassal's work.
- Every word spoken to the common people shall not be in dispute. People will talk with interest about what we know. People will hear about what we don't know and follow the path to learn that thing.
  An old proverb says:

  Cedar is straight, and pine bends.

  That is interesting and touches one's heart.
- One must think of loneliness. Make a friend of a man long dead before your birth. If you think you're lonely, open the writings of one's trade. Much urgent work lies inside.

The edict contained many articles, but this glimpse allows one to imagine questions such as, When did Kenshin take such interest in the cultivation of warriors? or With these ironclad rules throughout the clan, how can one train himself to silently prepare for emergencies?

Despite these ironclad rules and organization, neither the lord nor his vassals boasted about indifference toward them. Those ironclad rules also pulsated with the blood of humanity. The organization called the clan also connected man to man and soul to soul. Therefore, even the peculiarities of Demon Kojima Yataro were allowed to inhabit them. Although he was called *Trouble* until he became a man, everyone from his friends to his superiors thought, The time will come when he will be of use.

They sensed his shortcomings would be of service one day.

However, only Demon Kojima Yataro exhausted the slight friendliness around him. He had a wife but never stopped being a heavy drinker.

He also stepped outside the advice the warrior's code expressed by Kenshin. And a terrible thing happened one winter during a huge snowstorm typical of Echigo.

A large group of guards protected the moat around Kasugayama Castle and the areas near the gateways of Ninukido and San'nukido at the crossroad with Oote. Men from the guards' residence and the townsmen were called out. Light leaked out through the snow.

"Hey! Open the gate!" someone cried out while pounding frantically.

Inside were at least ten off-duty guards sitting in a circle and drinking. They had already drunk close to a half gallon that night.

"Don't open it. That sounds like Kojima."

"I don't want him in here. He'll drink everything."

"But those winds sound awful. We'll act like we don't hear him, then he'll go away."

They had a good time inside and didn't answer as they took out and put warm sake on the hearth. Outside, Yataro would go home.

"Hey! Hey! I'm freezing. Please let me in. Hey, why won't you open the door? Stop acting like you don't hear me. When I passed in front, that smell punched me in the nose, okay? How could I slide past down this snowy road? ... Don't be so mean. Dammit. Damn you."

Inside the house, they snickered and laughed. Yataro's knocks became more violent.

"You bunch of fools. I went to a lot of trouble to bring some food and nice gifts for you. It'll all go to waste after all this trouble ..."

He seemed to be telling the truth. Some of the men inside wondered, Is the food a trap? Had he worn them down? They opened the door and invited Yataro to join their circle.

Yataro drank to excess and had come empty-handed. He drank enough for five and lay on his side near the hearth snoring loudly.

"What a rude guy," one groused as they looked around at their dead-drunk drinking partner.

"This has become a habit."

They winked and nodded in agreement and roused Yataro from his sleep. Next, the warriors lied and outrageously scolded him.

"Give us the food. Hey, what happened to the gift?"

They ganged up on him.

"Where's the food?"

The unruffled Yataro said, "It's not here."

"So you lied? Apologize. Place both your hands on the ground and apologize for lying. If you don't, then kill yourself."

"It's simply not here. Nobody has to die."

"Well, go get it. Right now!"

"Okay, I'll get it. But you guys are ridiculous."

"What do you mean by ridiculous?"

"There wasn't even enough sake for me to get drunk. The food I'm going to bring is not for cheap sake like that. Go get some more, then I'll bring the food."

"Even if we don't get any more, there's still some sake left. We're not bringing it out until you get the food."

"What? There's more?"

"Get the food. If you don't, get down on the ground and apologize to all of us."

"What? ... You dopes. I'll get it now."

Yataro shakily stood and went out into the snow. A short time later, "Hey, I got it. How about this food? Have you ever eaten a delicacy like this anywhere in the world?"

He raised an object dangling from his hand from the entryway.

"Aah ...?"

A glance caused every last men to sober up in a heartbeat.

34

THE DUCK OF EARTHLY DESIRE

YATARO PRESENTED A duck from the moat. He gripped the duck's neck and lifted it above his head to show them.

Of course, the duck was dead. A little while ago, they heard a sound like a gunshot in the snowy winds. It appears he carried out the gun that had been lying on the large earthen floor. The shot may have come from that gun.

"Now you've done it...."

Each and every face was drained of color, and they all lost their appetite. The reason was plainly written on the notice board beside the moat.

Shooting ducks is strictly forbidden.

A common saying heard from Lord Kenshin was "the waterfowl in the moat are a strategic point."

Naturally, a violator would be put to death, a decision made in the time of the lord's father.

While going to the kitchen, Yataro looked down at a quiet crowd and asked, "Who's gonna make the stew? I'll pluck out the feathers and cook it."

He went out to the kitchen, plucked the feathers, loosened the meat from the bones, and prepared the duck on a large dish and returned.

But everyone was gone.

"... Hey, where'd they go?" he muttered but wasn't particularly surprised. He made the stew alone then ate and fell asleep.

Instead, at daybreak, government officials came. Yataro was tightly surrounded and walked off and into the castle.

He was pulled before Kenshin to be cross-examined.

"Why did you violate the prohibition?"

Yataro's answer was unremarkable.

"I'm always in and out of the castle and see so many of them. My greed wanted me to eat one just once. Because of my earthly desire, I decided to help myself to one."

Kenshin forced a smile. He should not have permitted this given only that reply. He would quibble over his life because he was Yataro. He was aware of this quibbling, but deep in Kenshin's heart, there was no desire to kill this important vassal over a duck. He would allow some sort of repentance.

In a short time, the disappearance of Yataro occurred while Kenshin journeyed to the capital. On the third year after his return to the clan, the first public act was forgiveness of his previous crime. Furthermore, the humanity of the man himself changed entirely during warrior training and put to use with his wisdom. Yataro gradually assumed responsible posts and accumulated acts of merit. Now as a commander, if "Hajikano Den'emon of Kai …" is spoken among the people in the world, "Demon Kojima Yataro in Echigo" immediately comes to mind.

35
THE FRAGRANT CHARIOT

AS AN ENVOY of the Takeda clan, Hajikano Den'emon entered the encampment on Mount Saijo to meet his old acquaintance Demon Kojima Yataro. Together, they climbed to the summit where Kanshin's headquarters stood. As much as they did not consider the other a friend or an enemy, they had a congenial chat as they walked. Yataro was said to admire this character but not only for personal reasons after being saved by him while he lurked around Kofu.

While in Kofu, Yataro asked himself what was Den'emon's natural disposition, because he privately recognized that "He is a warrior among warriors even in Kofu."

Around that time, this sort of rumor was found in talk traveling from the towns of Kofu.

In Tsutsujigasaki Yakata, Den'emon walked backward before the lord, the sword of a Buddhist priest had been placed in an adjacent room in the castle.

The priest was furious, Had Den'emon accidentally stepped on it? He was enraged.

The priest said to the row of samurai, "Was my soul kicked by someone's foot?"

The Buddhist priest was a cynical man. Because he did not have distinguished military service, he distrusted soldiers who did. He planned opposition by using his influence in the domestic administration. This sort of sentiment was common. Therefore, only this time he did not consent. In no way would he consent.

Den'emon said, "I'm sorry. I will lay both hands on the ground and apologize," and fell prostrate. Despite this, his companion monk argued with increasing ardor, "An apology is not enough."

When Den'emon eventually asked what should be done, he was told, "You kicked my sword. If I can't respond at least with a punch to your head, my feelings will not be calmed."

Remaining prostrate, Den'emon moved forward, "If it must be, please," then stuck out his head.

The priest punched him with all his might.

That is the story, but when the people of the castle town in Kofu heard this story through hearsay, they felt sympathy and said to themselves, "Just as I thought, he's a great man."

Thus, when Den'emon went out to the battlefield, everyone knew he was a brave warrior who stamped the crest of his helmet and the banners with the kanji for *Kyosha* (香車), the *Shogi* game piece for the Fragrant Chariot that only moves forward.

He was a man who pledged the spirit of driving forward of Kyosha stamped on his crest. Anyone would have immediately understood that the man was hard but feared the power of the priest whose fist should not have hit his head and would be called a man to be admired.

Many years later, he was turned into Kimura Shigenari in Osaka Castle in an anecdote to understand Shigenari's personality. However, some said the story about Den'emon had been told in private much earlier.

At any rate, at the battlefront on Mount Saijo, the envoy Hajikano Den'emon guided by Demon Kojima Yataro would finally meet Kenshin.

36
THE MAN IN THE EYESPOT

THE ENVOY WAS greeted by Kenshin's personal attendant Wada Kihei. The enemy's envoy who came here was waiting outside the military curtains.

"… Ah, it's quiet."

The envoy Den'emon escorted by Demon Kojima Yataro and another man stopped unexpectedly. He pretended to look up at the treetops and listen to the voices of the birds.

He secretly thought, It'll be good to have bloodstained clothes again. If his bloodthirsty presence and rage came, he imagined he'd become the fool.

The surrounding figures were quiet. Even seeing the shadows of the armor and the light of the spears and swords, the lone envoy was not threatened. It didn't feel like a false show of power.

The surroundings of the four-hundred-square-foot area enclosed by the curtains were cleanly raked. Kenshin's life resembled a quiet, secluded life in the mountains like the life of a hermit. Fallen pine needles were scattered on the pristine, swept ground.

Kenshin had camped here beginning on the sixteenth, and today was the twenty-eighth. During that time, rain fell and the winds blew. Consequently, the cedar bark and the cypress bark providing a roof for the temporary shelter but inadequate to shelter from the rain could be seen inside the enclosure.

"Envoy, we will withdraw into this place. The envoy greeter will no longer guide you. Where Kenshin is staying will soon come into view."

After completing their task, Yataro and his comrade returned to the base of the mountain. Den'emon was shown the way by Wada Kihei's hand along a path of bare ground missing the raked pattern.

"Please wait here," said Kihei. At last, the envoy Den'emon knew he was where Kenshin lived when he faced a thin cloth before his eyes.

He quietly sat on a shield given to him. A shield was a rug in camp; it was the seat taken by warriors. That is to say, they sat cross-legged on it.

"..."

The curtain before his eyes was taken down without a sound. Simultaneously, Den'emon bowed his head and only raised it again when he heard Kenshin's voice.

Kenshin said, "Are you Hajikano Den'emon, a vassal of the Takeda clan? Given the recent face-off of armies still without one battle, what business brings an earnest envoy to me? You seem to have hurried here with the purpose entrusted to you by Kizan Daikoji, the lord of the Koshu castle."

One more time, Den'emon was startled and bowed his head. His response did not reach panic. He guided himself to control several breaths from his depths and strained his eyes as he looked up to burn the figure of the man who he was seeing for the first time and also carried the Buddhist name Fushikian Kenshin.

37
FELLOWSHIP WITH A GUEST

KENSHIN SAT ON the camp stool on the grass and leaned his neat and orderly figure toward him.

He wore a sleeveless half-coat with chrysanthemum and paulownia patterns on the armor with black thread and laid down only a sheathed long sword. In the autumn sun shining between the trees, the gold fittings on his armor and the gold fittings of the long sword glinted each time his body swayed and dazzled the eyes.

Kenshin's look was not overwhelming. The hem of his greenish-brown Zen hood rested on his full cheeks. His tenderness and pupils were in harmony.

Above all, Den'emon's eyes were drawn to the portable seventeen-string koto placed in a corner near a small drum. His *fukikaeshi* helmet with its swept-back neck plates was set like an eternal treasure on an armored box made by the Myochin school.

Den'emon appraised the koto, the helmet, and the man.

No, that was secondary. He cautiously relayed his message as Shingen's envoy to Kenshin.

"The biggest regret is the challenge in the order from Lord Shingen. I presume there must be resentment over Warigatake, but I don't see any other path to resolve this matter. Your camp materialized in an instant; therefore, the agreement from the first year of Eiroku was already broken.... With this understanding, a Koshu company was also sent out in greeting to this land."

"Hmmm, ... well then," said Kenshin as his dimples appeared.

Den'emon with power in his voice said, "To Lord Shingen, this concerns what is called in these mountains and rivers in both the Koshu and Echigo clans the Storm of Bows and Arrows. Battles between mutual military strategies of men and horses have occurred three or four times and led to minor conflicts. Who knows how many dozen times, they were men mocked by the world and caused hardship to the peasants? This time, a great battle will easily break out. Lord Shingen repeatedly said to tell Lord Kenshin that the victor and the loser will be obvious."

"Oh, is that so? This is a long-cherished plan. When I agree, his returning home will be fine," said Kenshin.

"Since that is true, I visited without reserve. I crossed the Sai and Chikuma Rivers. The serious situation at your camp, your valor, and your unique courage and resourcefulness also filled the eyes of Lord Shingen. You are said to be happy to be born into a military family and to have a fine enemy. More than this, were you considering an attack to take Kaizu Castle? Again, my lord's order was to come here to ask if there was the desire to push the battle onto flat ground. Is the answer possibly yes?"

"This has been a recent concern. You speak of the Warigasake incident and this battlefield.

The greeter Wada Kihei and the elder general invited the envoy left behind to go outside and provided him with a seat in another shelter and treated him to food and drink.

"This is a gift from Lord Kenshin. There are few provisions in the camp, but this rivals a true *bento* lunch."

While being scrutinized as the envoy, Den'emon took the cup. Kihei offered side dishes on plain wood lacquered trays.

"Soon Demon Kojima will come for a leisurely talk with you," he said, then bowed and left.

38

FLOWERS ON THE DRY RIVERBED

THE SIDE DISHES he saw on the lacquered wooden tray were not local river fish or vegetables. They were from the seas near Echigo and delicacies from the snow country. Of course, the sake was not refined. However, their superb aroma could not be compared to the products of Kai and Shinano. To transport these products, large quantities had been loaded on the packhorses for carrying provisions.

Den'emon immediately reflected on this. Meanwhile, Demon Kojima Yataro came alone to be his host. He said, "Please, make yourself at home."

At first, Yataro seemed to be frank with him and said, "I know that you told my lord that I blended into life in the castle town Kofu years ago and was able to leave the province with ease because of you. That's why I came out on purpose to welcome you and renew an old friendship out of gratitude…. Again, I thank you, something I failed to say at the time. Thanks to you, I returned home to Echigo and undertook this service."

Den'emon said, "No, no, your thanks are a problem. I don't know how you'd know, but I have no memory of overlooking an enemy spy for even a moment. Your appearance simply changed. I recall a man who kneaded the earth in a blacksmith's home in Kofu. However, that sort of example tends to happen between friend and foe."

"Yes, yes, I remembered what you said. Don't you have several daughters?"

"Are you asking about my daughters?"

Den'emon was probably surprised. Yataro saw the glint in Den'emon's eyes. In the atmosphere of this battlefield and in the enemy camp as an envoy, it could be called panic to force himself but found absolutely no memory despite searching his entire body.

"My two eldest daughters have already married into other families. My other daughter has no suitor."

83

"No, there should be one," Yataro said and brought a full cup of sake to his smiling mouth then continued, "When I was in Kofu at that time, your cute, little daughter was not yet ten years old. I often remember seeing her in town and in the gardens of the shrine. But the years passed, I saw the same person in the castle town of Kasugayama. She somehow became a servant in the mansion of Kurokawa Osumi, a vassal of the Uesugi clan. You may have heard, with the assistance of someone who hailed from the region of Zenkoji Temple, she was employed as a lady's maid of a daughter in the Osumi clan.... Her name is Tsuruna. She has a mole near her lips on the left side. She looks like you."

"..."

"Den'emon, don't you remember the time you went on a pilgrimage to Zenkoji Temple and your daughter was left by the road? I would like to ask you where?"

The nerve of the big-boned warrior of a warring state revived Den'emon's courage this time. The cup of sake spilled from his hand and he burst out laughing.

"What you say brings back the memory. A few years ago, my youngest daughter went missing near Zenkoji Temple. So she ended up in Echigo. Your seeing her was a strange coincidence. She's surely at a fine age. Yes, I'd like to see her. I'll leave finding her whereabouts to divine will. She may be a lost child."

"Well, you are a brave father. If that is where your child is, you will also be welcome. Tsuruna is no longer in Echigo at the place I know of. She will soon leave to return to the air surrounding her parents and brothers. Regrettably, she went astray around here before she could step onto the land of Koshu. The next time, I pray the hands of her true parent will pick her up."

"What? Around here," said Den'emon unexpectedly and put down his cup. At that moment, he became the father of a child again. He moved forward squirming as if tethered to something that could not be broken.

He asked, "... Is that true? What you just said."

"What are you kidding?"

"Why is she in this area?"

"I don't know the details, but last evening, a young woman on a journey came wandering from somewhere on the dry riverbed facing Chikuma River. She asked for directions from Takeda's military porters busily cutting horse feed. A lookout stationed on Mount Saijo shows no mercy if he spots someone on the Takeda side. They lined up four or five guns and shot two workers. One shot hit Tsuruna. I was watching her from this mountain and ran down. I stopped the foot soldiers on lookout but was too late. I crossed the river to save her, but I waited and thought to return her to the other side of the river again. That may have been fortunate or unfortunate for Tsuruna. I went around daybreak today, but her fallen body was gone. According to the foot soldiers, the peasant laborers cutting grass were confused in the evening twilight and somehow carried her off escaping to some far-off place.... Even if wounded, she may still be alive. I thought about that from the morning and, coincidentally, about you the envoy from the enemy army on the opposite shore. It's not chance. She may have attained Buddhahood at Zenkoji Temple.... Military work has no free time. If I had a spare moment, I'd wonder if she were treated in one of the peasant homes in Kawanakajima near this area. I'd visit them, no, I'd ask Providence to lend a hand."

Yataro took the sake bottle to fill the envoy's cup and his own. The cups piled up.

Den'emon sprung from his seat.

"I'm being spoiled by your kind attention. I've had enough. Please give my regards to the lord."

"Are you going home?"

"My wretchedness here is unforgivable. I fear I've stayed too long.... I don't know how to express my thanks for your courtesy from the beginning. If I remove this armor, I will be a dead man instead of a parent in the world. Surely, when dressed in armor, before my eyes, the deaths of parents, a wife's tears, and a child's blood will be seen, and nothing will be remembered. There is only a personal battle. Therefore, I will apologize now. We exchanged drinks here today, but tomorrow, I will meet you in the area where the Sai and Chikuma rivers flow as Hajikano Den'emon carrying a spear that will not be blunt."

"Don't worry. In that case, I will be Demon Kojima Yataro," he said with a smile and stood, "I will see you off to the foot of the mountain."

39

FANTASY AND REALITY

THE ENVOY'S BOAT with the parasol held high again crossed the waters of the Chikuma to return to the opposite shore.

The atmosphere of the camp of the Koshu army in the distant, hazy band at the crossing near Amenomiya somehow anticipated the return of the envoy alerted by the sounds of the winds blowing through the thicket of banners.

When a voice promptly reported to Shingen with the central troops, "Lord Hajikano has returned," the air in the curtained field headquarters livened up. Den'emon passed straight through and dropped to his knees a distance from Shingen and his clan members and various generals.

"… Well, what happened?" asked Shingen.

Den'emon gave a blunt answer to the blunt question and his report. Without pausing, he explained, "The enemy camp is extraordinarily calm. I can infer from Kenshin's brow that he expects certain victory. Again, all the officers and men pledged their lives to leave their country. The camp was orderly, discipline was flawless. I did not see one tangled thread. By piecing together the above and making an inference, the positions taken on Mount Saijo are not the result of his recklessness or lack of ingenuity. Yet, I don't believe a well-planned military strategy exists. That could be called a plan without a plan and rules without rules. The battle formation is stark. Shock troops willing to risk their lives are being readied. Otherwise, I shouldn't feel any deception like a Zen temple in the central army commanded by Kenshin. Truth quickly follows a lie. For a moment there, I felt squeezed from both sides by lies and the truth and shuddered. No raiding party like a night attack or morning assault will come out at all. Whether surrounded by the truth or trapped in a climate of lies, all will not live to return home."

Of course, he candidly relayed these words and Kenshin's response.

Shingen said nothing and listened to the entire report. The blood vessels beside his ear hole sprouting hair swelled.

Until sunset, Shingen's camp was in an uproar. It was positioned opposite the central force on Mount Saijo. In the curtained field headquarters where Shingen was, his clan and the star generals in Kai were in deliberation. Men came and went one after another. Even the horses outside the camp were not as unruly as the commotion here.

The inky autumn night sky appeared in the world of only the sounds of insects and stars. Takeda's banners would slowly emerge soon after smoke rose from the cooking like haze from the camps. They faced upstream on the Chikuma River. Originally, the enemy on Mount Saijo must have seen them when they looked closely. When moving toward the flank, they must intend to raise a torrent of bullets from the opposite shore and stage a valiant attack at some time with the cavalry kicking up sprays of water. While their preparations were adequate, the very dangerous expulsion force was seen by the enemy.

They wondered whether the winding black flow was wider and longer than the depth of the Chikuma River. In the dead of night, a part of the vanguard was already wading across in the area of the tributary to the Chikuma and the wide rapids.

"... Shingen, I know what you're thinking," Kenshin surely muttered on Mount Saijo. It was difficult to guess whether the Koshu force beginning to wade across the flow of the wide rapids would immediately send the entire force to Kaizu Castle. For now, when they entered the castle, their number would be met by the number of their allies, Kousaka Danjo's men. Furthermore, his troop strength was large and would respond on Mount Saijo by using all of Shingen's ingenuity and preparation, but Kenshin vividly knew this, like counting the stars in the Big Dipper, in his heart.

40
ISLANDS ON LAND

TO THE STRATEGIC eye, if the plain is seen as an ocean, the scattered hills and mountains are seen as islands on the ocean, and the value of their use can be considered.

Kenshin's encampment was on Mount Saijo and quickly became the forward base because of its geographical advantages. Shingen swept the camp from the plain and entered Kaizu Castle. His actions were driven by the thought of a siege army in danger on this stark land. This meant the castle could be regarded as an island. Human labor added a fortified port at a steep area on the shore.

Kaizu Castle was bounded on three sides by mountains and faced west toward the plain like a port entry. The Chikuma River flowed below forming a large, natural outer moat.

"You cannot talk about castles without ever seeing Kaizu Castle" was often said among military men at the time who were passionate about castle fortification techniques.

The famous general of Kai, Baba Shouyu Nobuharu, was said to have come by his title Shouyu, junior assistant minister, as the result of a troublesome arrest. No, his title was the idea of Yamamoto Kansuke.

In any case, the noteworthy man always silent concerning the country of Echigo was Takeda.

As seen by Takeda, the army he took each time to the field far from this border was not an ordinary army. Therefore, there was a need to position regular fortress soldiers. A base was set up when a large army came out and played a crucial role for storing food provisions, horse feed, and stores of ammunition and weapons for a siege army.

Naturally, Uesugi also needed to maintain these conditions. Compared to the distance from Kofu to this place, the distance from Uesugi's home country was much shorter, but the road conditions were extremely poor and did not change even for a foreign war away from his home province.

Thus, he also had a stronghold on Mount Tabusa in the north of Minochi-gun. But Kenshin abandoned this base far behind and went south deep into enemy territory.

The castle on Mount Asahi was between Zenkoji Temple and the Sai River nearer to the battlefield than the fort on Mount Tabusa. In spite of the great need for a base there for support, Kenshin abandoned it.

Initially, Shingen set up camps from Mount Chausa to the Amenomiya crossing. Despite this cutting off Asahi Castle from Mount Saijo, Kenshin preferred to meet death on Mount Saijo. His isolation could only be seen as an honor. By that day, half of his forty years had been spent mostly on the battlefield, but Shingen had never seen an enemy like this and did not understand this sort of military strategy.

41
THE MILITARY STRATEGY
OF THE WOODPECKER

BEYOND THE RAVINE floated a milky white haze. Something between mist and rain showers was falling.

Shingen fixed his eyes and said, "What does the military division know? Tell me straight."

His eyes resembled amber jewels. Today, another military evaluation centered on the movements of those eyes.

The interior of Kaizu Castle felt like the gloomy air in the inner cavern of the Great Buddha. Although daytime, candles were scattered around and flickering dimly.

The rows of clan members, seasoned warriors, and the lord of the castle Kousaka Danjo attending the deliberation were qualified men but only in an extremely limited realm.

Obu Hyobu Toramasa was a brave general called the Fierce Tiger of Kai. In line with his name, he did not waffle when seeking a statement from Shingen. He said, "This idle siege army and these daily war councils are useless to me."

"Useless?"

"They only drain fighting morale. When your fighting force of eighteen thousand men hits the front with Kofu, it will crush Mount Saijo in a rush forward and in a stroke eagerly enter without pushing forward to the Echigo territory. However, confusion strangely appears when the camp easily changes for no reason, the enemy is spied on, and Kenshin's heart is gauged. Then attacks on this castle will come, and time will be spent in daily war councils like this. As usual, the soldiers will get bored."

Hyobu's words were blunt. The sullen Shingen listened with his thick chin tilted slightly up. He looked as if he were waiting for his next words, And so?

Hyobu spoke in a raised voice, "If the heartless shadow is looked at as consequential, various elements are understood. Surrounding the enemy's Mount Saijo and gauging Kenshin's heart, like the shadows of a moonlit night resemble suspicion and fear of all evil spirits. When I look, I believe Kenshin has no plan. His lack of a plan may lead us to think of him as an ally. We will suddenly cast a shadow that can be likened to a grueling task when he is not understood."

"Yes, that makes sense."

Shingen didn't dare scold him and offered no counterargument. He slowly turned to look at Sanada Yukitaka and asked, "What do you think?"

Yukitaka answered in few words, "I better understand Lord Hyobu's explanation."

Shingen faced his younger brother beside him and repeated the question.

"What do you think, Shoyoken?"

Takeda Shoyoken supported Obu Hyobu's explanation for the most part and said, "The reinforcements of the large force from the front at Echigo may come by chance and cut off the rear of the enemy, or an unanticipated military strategy will emerge. And all movements will be outmaneuvered," then he added, "Also, Shinshu is already under the power of Koshu. Kenshin projected his base camp deep into Shinshu and boasts of a far greater number of troops than his enemy. But our Koshu force is slow and will interfere for some time but will be unable to take action. Kenshin's ability may seem frightening. That may in some way reflect the public sentiment in the various districts of Shinshu. So the sooner the decision, the better."

"Uh-huh," said Shingen, nodded, and then said to himself, In the war councils, I could always count on the elder Obata Yamashiro Nyudo for valuable advice, but he fell ill and died. And Harami-no-Kami was gravely wounded last year at the destruction of Warigatake. The loss of their words saddens me. I will ask Douki, What do you think?

Shingen turned to face Yamamoto Kansuke Nyudo Douki. Kansuke was a strong elder. The honesty of the senior counselors was often in conflict with Shingen. Therefore, Shingen frequently took decisive action and pressed forward. This led to deeply cautious elders.

On this day, however, the situation was reversed. The usually aggressive Shingen showed no signs of moving. Yamamoto Douki always offered half-hearted advice but today fully opened his mouth to make specific recommendations.

"A little while ago someone argued that the enemy has no plan. I agree that this is the end. But his lack of a plan differs greatly from not having a plan because of ignorance or recklessness. I think Kenshin will gamble life and death in this battle and live to walk again in his birthplace in the mountains of Echigo. His frightening, desperate lack of a plan can be viewed as a win followed by a walk back home. Will the resolve of the allies cause them to act with urgency until they equal him? Knowing that, leaving matters to the wishes of the man who should hesitate will bring immediate destruction and present our allies with only one course of action."

"But an uncertain man would go for the fast war and a quick resolution."

"All right ..." he said and looked in turn at each man's face, "It is decided."

"Good."

Shingen adjusted his thick kneecaps again and, for the first time, announced his decision.

"Only during today's deliberation, I saw that Kenshin has no plan whatsoever. If the corpse of Kenshin himself is buried in this land, I will also cheerfully have no regrets of going off to war. Douki, what do you think about trying the Woodpecker Strategy?"

"You said the Woodpecker Strategy? Your insight is keen. I know that the enemy is quite peculiar this time."

At that moment, a shout could be heard beside the moat outside the castle. The seated Kousaka Danjo wondering what was happening stood and stuck his head through a narrow gap to look down. Shingen and all the generals were silent for a short time as they stared at his back.

"They're irritable.... Are the ally's foot soldiers arguing again?" asked Oyamada Bitchu-no-kami from behind. Danjo pulled his head back in and shook it no.

"No, no, the scouting unit that secretly went out the night before last was substantially diminished. The remaining seven or eight who returned to the castle gate were bruised and had light wounds. Their condition was the result of going fairly deep into enemy territory to surround the outposts of Uesugi's power and barely managing to make their way back. I will get the details and report back," said Danjo who left in a hurry after receiving permission from Shingen.

42
PLAYING THE KOTO

THE EXCHANGE AMONG the scouts was heated.

They risked death but found no way to advance close to the enemy's headquarters to uncover the enemy's core.

The usual scout units went out with fewer than the original number, just one or two men in some cases.

However, not one of the scouts from Kaizu Castle returned alive.

The night before last, Kousaka Danjo sent out a squad of twenty-five scouts. They annihilated any enemy patrol they encountered and were able to break through the sentry line. If things went well, they hoped to reach the headquarters on Mount Saijo and receive information from one or two scouts.

"Mataroku, have they returned?" called out Danjo as he descended the tower to the lead scout Takaido Mataroku in a nearby room in the castle and pressed for a report.

Mataroku's left hand was injured, and his elbows were wrapped in rags like grafts.

"We crossed Tadagoe and went as far as Omura but …"

"What? You only made it as far as Omura."

"We were surrounded by an enemy ambush and attacked without mercy. Eventually, only seven managed to escape."

"Were they all later killed in battle?"

"No, two disguised themselves earlier as peasants and took a big detour from the mountain where Hosenji Temple sits and hid near Dokuchi. If they survive and return, then we will find out about the situation on Mount Saijo," said a discouraged Danjo.

Soldiers were lost, and the objective had not been achieved. There was no information to present to the war council before Shingen. At daybreak two days later, the lone scout no longer expected to return had returned. This man performed the meritorious deed of separating from Mataroku's scouts and taking a detour through the mountains to successfully spy on the headquarters on Mount Saijo.

While he took great pains to enter the tiger's mouth and learned hard-to-get knowledge about the enemy's actual situation, unfortunately, the scout who carried out this deed was a woodcutter born in a neighboring district and, honestly, was a dimwit. Therefore, his answers to Danjo's questions were too scattered and irrelevant.

The following questions and his answers give a sense of this.

"Did you go to Mount Saijo?"

"Yes. I went."

"To what area on Mount Saijo?"

"I walked in all directions from the top of the mountain."

"Why didn't the enemy capture you?"

"I don't know. I wondered that too"

"What was on Mount Saijo?"

"A lot of Uesugi warriors."

"If you walked from the peak, you probably saw the main camp where Kenshin is."

"Yes, a little. I spent one night on the peak."

"Did you see the headquarters?"

"At midnight, I heard the sounds of a koto and thought that was strange. I made my way there by moving silently from shadow to shadow of the trees."

"The sound of a koto? … What are you talking about? Didn't you see that in a dream?"

"Me too. I thought it was a dream at first. But when I looked, General Kenshin was kneeling and playing a small, portable koto. This isn't a dream, I thought."

"Where did you see this?"

"In the headquarters where the bonfires burned."

"Was Kenshin alone at midnight playing the koto?"

"No, he wasn't. A young general, a gray-haired general, and maybe five or six men moved back toward the hem of the curtain of the field headquarters. All of them were nodding off, crying, or their heads were dropping down."

"You probably heard Kenshin playing the koto."

"Maybe."

"What did Kenshin say to his vassals?"

"He played the koto, gazed at the moon in the overcast sky, and in a soft voice, recited a poem."

"Were all the samurai in the camp lively?"

"The horses were neighing a lot."

"I don't care about the horses. What was the fighting spirit?"

"I don't really know."

"Are there provisions for the soldiers or not?"

"No."

"Nothing?"

"Nothing."

"You don't know whether their fighting morale is high or whether there are provisions."

"If I saw the foot soldiers and samurai eating, it wasn't brown rice but millet porridge or rice porridge. Bones of the packhorses had been thrown out. They're eating horse meat. I saw that somewhere on the mountain. There were no bags of beans or rice."

"How did you get back without being wounded?"

"I returned far downstream from Amenomiya on the side facing Hachimanbara and took my time walking back."

No matter how shrewd the questions were, the results were at this level.

When Shingen heard this by hearsay, he said, "That man is a warrior."

Then he ordered a substantial reward; he had gained a hint of information about uncertain enemy movements. He seemed satisfied with having learned something.

The month passed and the beginning of September came. On the sixteenth of the past month, the Uesugi army set up camp and had been here for twenty days. Unless provisions for the troops were carried to that mountain, the beginnings of dwindling provisions can be imagined.

The last-ditch, risky positions of his troops will drain a great deal of their spirit. The spirit of urgency lasted an instant. When that sharp fighting spirit left, earthly passions returned.

The men under Kenshin felt nihilistic at battle positions with no plan. They felt ashamed, remembered fear, could not go back in retreat, could not go forward in an advance, and would become corpses buried in a stretch of Mount Saijo. Shingen thought that was the truth.

Their annihilation did not have to be immediate. The best plan may have been to let a few days pass. The Woodpecker Strategy he planned in secret was distributed without any mistakes and would finally have a satisfactory effect. Diligent research and preparations began on the allotment of troops, the deployment of the commanding officers, the schedule, the movements, and the geographic advantages.

The Woodpecker Strategy involved the woodpecker hitting its beak against the tree bark to frighten swarms of bugs hiding in the hollow of the tree and not inclined to go outside. This tactic forces them out in huge numbers from the front to be gulped down into the stomach as food. The so-called wisdom of the woodpecker was the philosophy and would carry out a war of mass slaughter that will shake Heaven and Earth.

43
THIRTEEN THOUSAND TEARS
IN A WHITE PEARL

WEARINESS COMES EASILY in a siege army.

The strong soldiers of the enemy do not easily battle boredom. Interest is lost in weariness.

At times, the enemy at the center like a fog boiling up from this listlessness whispered discontent and invited winces. All the flaws of the samurai attendants gave rise to discord and brought thoughts of home to mind. The weak points of all earthly desires were struck. The fighting spirit of the Iron Wall gathered in utter confusion.

A day is long on the battlefield. For twenty days or a month, the opposing armies took up positions. Their soldiers with bated breath were not fighting on the outside. In fact, inside each of their hearts, the fight was more than the battle.

Victory is ours!

The fight was here. It was a daily, quiet, bitter struggle more difficult than beating another enemy, demanded more furious energy, and hardened as the siege lengthened.

Mysteriously, however, this sedimentation was not visible in the soldiers on Mount Saijo.

Invigorating autumn was sent everyday. On rainy and foggy days, the hearts of more than thirteen thousand men congealed into one mass to become smoke within the dreariness. Is this an immobile body? The morning cleared by the sun in the morning mist resembling steam rising from the spirits of the entire force as one.

There was no reason.

The endless bewilderment caused by weariness, homesickness, and dread acted on their persistence in serving despite relatively many concerns about the safety of their lives. The central troops more than the vanguard, and the rear troops more than the central troops felt that way.

However, there was no vanguard or home front on Mount Saijo. The distance to the enemy Kaizu Castle was a short two and a half miles away. If viewed from the mountain on a sunny day, its white walls and banners were vividly seen. It resembled the glistening fog of life in which life on that morning does not know the evening and a dream in the grass connected to the evening does not know the morning. Mysteriously, that scene was no more than the pleasant idea of a normal day without incident. Each of the approaching lives was like a polished white pearl. All the persistent confusion was thrown off; instead, they lived with openhearted, naive smiling faces. Not to mention, on only this day this autumn, the party of Uesugi warriors from Echigo who constantly competed to improve had no reason to stifle the progress of samurai whose lives were more than lives in times like these.

44
A CHRYSANTHEMUM BRANCH

"**DON'T GET MAD** Gonroku."

"I'm all right."

"Well, do you want me to do it?"

"No, there's only a little more."

Gonroku turned and poked his head into the hole he had been digging. He answered his master from inside the hole.

Demon Kojima Yataro leaned in with him and peeked from the side into the hole having a diameter of just two feet. Gonroku's hand scratched at the ground like a chicken at his feet.

At that moment, someone was walking toward them with a soft rustling among the trees behind them. The crimson leaves of the sumac trees danced on the stranger's shoulders.

"Yataro, what are you doing?" asked a surprised voice, and the pair turned around.

Gonroku raised his head from the hole. Both hands and his face were caked with mud. He was startled and looked slightly guilty then jumped back and lay prostrate.

"Ah, is that you, Lord?" remarked the slightly baffled Yataro, "I was pretty bored and dug up some yams. When this foot soldier becomes good at digging up yams, I will brag and know I'll get much stronger."

Kenshin forced a laugh. He was at the cliff directly below headquarters but came alone without even a page. He approached to peek into the yam hole, he said, "Of course, yams. It took patience to dig. Well, dig all you wish."

"Thank you. Is there a goblin like this underground? In this camp over several seasons, the creatures above ground seemed to have eaten everything edible. The akebia fruits, walnuts, hackberries, wild grapes, and even the sprouts.... Yataro, is anything left?"

"Yes, there is. If you'd like to eat, there are grass roots and even dirt."

"Uh-huh …" he nodded with a smile and said, "Is everyone at the foot of the mountain in good spirits?"

"Despite being alone, I'm not bored … but why are you walking alone?"

"Like you, I'm walking to stave off boredom. I came out to look for wild chrysanthemums, but few seem to be on this mountain."

"Is that so?"

"… I haven't found any."

"I've seen them at the foot of the mountain. You should search there."

"Really! One branch would be splendid. If I find one, I'll bring it here."

"Later, I will bring you a branch and yams."

"You will bring me yams?"

"They will be a gift."

"In that case, I'll be delighted to accept them. I'll also be waiting for that branch of wild chrysanthemums."

When Kenshin retraced his steps, alone again he leisurely climbed toward the level ground of the encampment on the mountain called the camp flats.

45

THE CHRYSANTHEMUM FESTIVAL

THE AUTUMN DAY was clear during the morning, but clouds began to gather around noon. Myoko and Kurohime were distant mountains shrouded in fog. Over the past few days, the weather in the plateau was uncertain, but the waters in the Chikuma River directly below and the Sai River further away appeared to be flooding.

"That's good. Tell everyone to come," came Kenshin's order from inside the fluttering curtains of the field headquarters in the winds carrying signs of rain showers.

The attendant answered promptly and ran off.

He was headed to the camps of the military units divided among several locations on the mountain. The invited generals soon came to this place. They were Naoe Yamato-no-kami, Kakizaki Izumi-no-kami, Amakasu Oumi-no-kami, and Nagao Totou-no-kami, only the senior vassals of the field headquarters.

The generals entered and looked astonished. The reason was a wide straw woven mat was spread out. Also, a lacquered plain wooden tray and a cup were provided at each place. At times to celebrate taking to the field or a winning army, kelp and chestnut were placed on the lacquered tray on the tray table. Persimmons in vinegar dressing and side dishes of steamed dried fish could be seen. A small bit, truly a tiny amount, of yam was grated on top.

"I know the reason for the invitation.... But will this be a joyous banquet?" asked Amakasu Oumi-no-kami.

After all ten seasoned warriors saw the place settings, Kenshin smiled amiably and said, "They say time slips away in the mountains. A month has passed and today is September 9 exactly twenty-five days since we left the castle on Mount Kasuga on the fourteenth day of last month.... Before we realized it, we became a siege army in for the long haul. Everyone is eager for war day and night but tired. But at the same time, today is the day we should

100

celebrate and enjoy. It's not much with so little rice, but let's exchange cups. Make yourselves comfortable and enjoy the sake."

First, the generals drank in the sentiment of Kenshin's words and warmed their hearts before their lips touched the cups.

Naoe Yamato-no-kami asked, "You wish this day to be one of enjoyment, but what are we celebrating? ..."

"No, no," said Kenshin shaking his head, "Have you all forgotten? The auspicious day of September 9 is the Chrysanthemum Festival. Since ancient times, this day has been the day for viewing chrysanthemums."

"Oh! ..."

Each man slapped his knees.

"That's true. That's true. Sir, today was the seasonal festival of the chrysanthemum."

For the first time, the men's eyes were drawn to the sutra-reading desk with one leg in the center of the straw mat. One branch of yellow wild chrysanthemums was inserted in a copper flower vase of a small crane's head. They finally realized that branch did not have the simple meaning of a chrysanthemum.

Kenshin often said, "The ninth day of the ninth month, nine is a positive number. The purpose of the Chrysanthemum Festival is to be festive and joyful. A characteristic of the chrysanthemum is its longevity. This tale has been handed down in China, too. One day, a legendary wizard peeked into the house of Koukei in Runan, China, and said, 'This autumn will bring disaster. If you think you won't escape, put cornelian cherries in a crimson silk sack, hang it from your elbow, and climb a high mountain.' As predicted, that year, a plague hit many in Koukei's village. Every last chicken and dog collapsed. Only the house of Koukei had no deaths. From the Heian era to this morning, whether from the floor of the Imperial Palace, the clans in the four classes of workers — scholars, farmers, artisans, merchants — chrysanthemums are viewed to bring joy to their hearts, chrysanthemum sake is drunk, and their bodies are nurtured. I have the habit of saying, 'I'll be happy if the climb is high today.' ... I am not searching but am on the land of Mount Saijo. Most of all, a lifetime of one day is blessed by sunlight, just like health. Shouldn't you enjoy yourselves? Let us celebrate."

The cups were filled to the brim.

As much as possible, the spirits of the generals united to find the truth in the melancholy of the long siege.

All the generals raised their cups as they gazed at the chrysanthemums. The talk flowed, and the gloom was lifted. They could not help not wanting to depart and feeling a touch of sorrow.

"Lord ... I may sound stupid but forgive me," said Naoe Yamato-no-kami as if he could no longer hold back something he wanted to say, Nagao Totou-no-kami on his right urged him from the corner of his eye. Without exception, the eyes of all the others focused on Kenshin's face.

Kenshin's almond-shaped eyes were suddenly red. Everyone in the group, including him, put down their cups.

"Sanetsuna, is there something you wish to say?" Kenshin asked then gave his full attention.

46
ADVICE FOR THE LORD

NAOE YAMATO-NO-KAMI SANETSUNA was an experienced general among experienced generals and the third generation to serve Kenshin and his forefathers.

His ability and loyalty were recognized by all. Moreover, Kenshin had an unusual faith and love for him. Nevertheless, since going to war this time, this veteran had not made one attempt to offer advice, nor had Kenshin sought him out for counsel.

Given this situation with Yamato-no-kami, Kenshin had not sought advice from any of the other generals either. And with each passing day, the awful conditions at this dangerous location of the encampment worsened. Staying for one day was said to increase the danger by one day. Reality closed in as thirteen thousand lives would starve or gravestones would be laid down at this place.

"What does your gut say about an advance or a retreat from this place? The circumstances do not cast the slightest doubt on the always valiant and courageous vassals, but our rations are already gone. Today ..."

"Is that so?" asked Kenshin who then very gently gave an unusual scolding.

"If that's the case, I often repeated from the time we first took up position here that I am a blank, flawless man who has no plan or has a plan that resembles having no plan. There's no need to repeat that over and over. In a word, do you understand?"

"Yessir ..." said the generals moved by his words. Yamato-no-kami persisted, "With all due respect, how does the great heart of our lord not understand that the vassals will pledge our lives? As you've said, the enemy Shingen has occupied Kaizu Castle since the twenty-fourth of last month, has been preparing for war, and stocked its provisions. Our allies are surely growing tired of the siege. If there is just one unguarded moment, he is alert enough to achieve certain victory with a spectacular shock. In other words, I am cautious about gauging the long-awaited opportunity. By considering the past actions of the allies, and the shipment of provisions for our soldiers being planned now at Zenkoji Temple, one certainty is a sneak attack by Takeda's force will be carried out at that time. And as I've said many times before they have cut off those routes and made the exchange of letters with the home province impossible. Not to mention the food, our rank-and-file soldiers are already eating dead horses and boiling tree bark, and no complaints are heard even from the hatamoto. That tragic patience will not continue forever. With some drastic change in your wisdom, I am asking you to act with discretion. Over the several days of this gathering, we have worried constantly only over this matter. The truth is we discussed in private how to ask this favor."

"Is it that serious? … Well, everyone seems to have a restless nature. In that case, let me ask a question. You told me your opinion earlier. Tell me, what will bring victory?"

"We foolishly drove our force too deep into Mount Saijo. The enemy's larger force is based in Kaizu and has managed to occupy various routes. Although a rapid change would be quite difficult, today, I don't think we're out of resources yet."

"Strangely, shouldn't we stay the course?"

"In that case, better than cowering here forced to eat our dwindling and already scant food provisions, wouldn't the better option be to launch a magnificent frontal attack to corner the enemy in Kaizu Castle. Each part of the enemy's scattered army along various routes would be destroyed. By far, this war will be considered glorious."

Kenshin said, "No, no, if we attack Kaizu, that attack will occur before Shingen leaves for Kofu. Even if he comes like a sudden shower, and the rear guard consists of the powerfully built men of Kofu, our allies would be defeated. I have been holding back but will boldly choose that fierce battle."

"If that is a disadvantage and your will is reckless, going to war this time will stop at making preparations. For now, the return to camp after the battle is expected to be next spring. How will the force go to battle again?"

"That is not my will."

"I may be needlessly worrying about this matter, but Takeda's army is twice the size of the allies. A portion is holed up in Kaizu, but what if the rest unexpectedly raced to Echigo and encircled the castle on Mount Kasuga,…"

"Aha, ha, ha, ha. It will be interesting if that happens. If Shingen attacks Echigo, then my easy task will be to storm Kofu and conquer his government seat. However, during my absence on Mount Kasuga, twenty thousand soldiers and a year's worth of arrows and bullets were put in storage. How can that impertinent Shingen not see what's before his eyes?"

At some time, the sun began to set. Dusk came fast inside the curtains of the field headquarters. Under the clouds of scattered rain showers falling of the chilly setting sun, the generals did not brighten but frowned and stood. Eventually, Kenshin's words and that day died without a plan. At an unknown moment, voices ceased in the camp. Under two watch fires and the shimmering evening twilight, the only sounds were the faint taps of leaves falling like rain.

47

DISTANT SMOKE

The emperor, a child of the god of heaven,
His reign will come generation after generation.
A bright spirit is not concealed.
Tradition slips by.
By tradition, no, in succession.
A story told by those who saw,
A warning from those who heard.
A new, fresh name.
Thoughts lazily come.
Lies and the end of a parent's name,
A burden on the clan name Otomo, a brave servant.

DURING THE EVENING of the Chrysanthemum Festival on the ninth day of the ninth month, Kenshin gave the impression of slight intoxication. After the evening meal, he placed the portable koto on his knees and plucked the seven strings with his fingers as he hummed an old poem from the *Man'yoshu* by Otomo Kojihi, Governor of Izumo.

After being dismissed from office, Otomo wrote *A Parable for the Clan* to the sons of his clan to stress the virtue of loyal service.

The pine firewood in the bonfires crackled and popped open in the rain showers.

They were not very wet. The night moon of the Chrysanthemum Festival from the rain clouds fell scattered and mingled with the tree leaves to shine a pale light on the mountains and rivers.

His eyebrows jumped and he said, "Ah, the voices of wild geese."

White moonlight lit Kenshin's face.

Both the senior samurai and young samurai holding back the hems of the curtains looked up. The lord's lips drew into a line and he stopped playing.

"Yes? … Who is it?"

Kenshin's gaze stopped at the human shadow resembling a crow high up in a large tree above the camp.

As night turned to day, allied lookouts kept a constant watch on Kaizu Castle. He noticed a man who seemed to have that role and gave the order, "Summon that man."

The senior samurai understood, rushed out, and soon returned with the lookout stationed in the tree. Kenshin himself good-naturedly called over the man to question him. The little space between them led the man to dread censure for some error.

"On nights like this, what is the view of Kaizu Castle?" Kenshin asked this simple question in a kind voice.

The lookout's tension eased and he replied, "I can barely see the castle when the moon is out, and when the moon is hidden, I can see next to nothing."

"Yes, I see," said Kenshin smiling, "It is a great duty to always be in the tree. Has anything changed tonight in the direction of Kaizu?"

"No, sir. Nothing has changed."

"All right. What about the dry riverbed of the Chikuma River?"

"Earlier, I saw unusual smoke hanging in the air from the west gate of the castle to the low part of the riverbed. At first, I thought it was the evening haze."

"Smoke?"

"Yes sir."

"And now? Can you still see it?"

"It's still faintly rising. When I thought about it, I knew it was smoke from cooking the evening meal. On a cloudy, rainy night like tonight, smoke stays low when it rises from the castle wall, so at first, I thought it was a little weird. ..."

"Very good. Leave!"

This time Kenshin's voice was close to a roar. Perhaps stunned by a thought, the koto fell from his knees. Kenshin said nothing as he stood and his long strides took him outside the curtains.

48
MOMENTS OF LIGHT AND DARK

KENSHIN STOOD still.

He climbed to the edge of a spur at a slightly higher elevation than the position of the troop headquarters in the encampment and stood frozen in place for a long time.

Several generals and hatamoto scrambled up to him from inside a nearby curtained enclosure and asked, "What's happening?" as they squatted near him.

"…"

Just short of two-and-a-half miles upstream on the Chikuma and Sai rivers from their position stood Kaizu Castle. One view was the entire plain of a wide basin extending for a stretch from the distant mountains to the foot of Mount Saijo.

"…?"

Kenshin's eyes focused and fixed on the far-off point of Kaizu Castle.

However, the rainy evening was dark and overcast.

The moon peeked out from between the clouds, and in an instant, dark clouds shut it out. The flickering never stopped making Heaven and Earth dark and light.

"Is Suruga here? Usami?"

"I'm here."

"Bring Naoe and Amakasu," commanded Kenshin to those behind him.

Usami Suruga-no-kami, Naoe Yamato-no-kami, and Amakasu Oumi-no-kami rushed to his side and looked at his face. Kenshin's eyes remained focused on the distance and did not glance at any of the men who came.

"Lord…. What is it? Has something unusual been discovered tonight among the enemy at Kaizu?"

"There. Look there."

The moonlight shined from Kenshin's face onto the mountains and the

108

rivers. Even Kenshin's pointing hand was white.

"From a little while ago until now, smoke has been rising at Kaizu. It's a little early to be cooking the evening meal. The smoke that eventually shrouded the area was too much for daily cooking. Thinking about it, they may be preparing provisions for tomorrow and the day after tomorrow. Surely within the night, they intend to send out the huge army from Kaizu Castle to start the war. Wonderful. This is great. The time has come," Kenshin concluded then added, "We will prepare, too."

He smiled and, in fact, was quite pleased.

No plan was not simply the absence of a plan. He breathed out in relief because he had been waiting for this chance. The *pause* was gauged while pounding the drum, and the *pause* was required in all entertainment. Great patience in military tactics was found in the *pause*.

"There will be no mistakes in the defense preparations. If the enemy comes, and I hope they do, they will not make it far enough to set foot on the first or second stage of the stockade, and will only be massacred."

Both Usami and Amakasu immediately grasped the defense protections and defensive fighting.

When they interpreted what he said as get ready, Kenshin shook his head no and faintly smiled.

"This place is a temporary foothold and was nothing more than a scaffold to wait for a change. He has already shown change, and I have a position to take. Generally, defense protections and defensive fighting are not passive. My hope is to not change even a little after leaving Mount Kasuga. In other words, they will persist in rushing in on the offensive and carry Kenshin's camp into Shingen's camp."

Next, Kenshin searched for his brush-and-ink case, grabbed his writing brush and began to write down the plan for taking to the field and what to look for in several items.

He handed the order to a few of the generals and said, "Immediately distribute this order to the soldiers under command."

49

ECCENTRIC AND JUST

WRITTEN MILITARY ORDERS are martial law.

This time, Kenshin dashed off the following.

- Until the allied soldiers are reached, provisions shall be put to immediate use.
- All remaining objects shall be carried in waist packs provided for provisions. One day's allotment for tomorrow is sufficient.
- With regard to a previous problem, armor shall not sag. Bind straw sandals tightly. Special tools shall be the responsibility of those skilled in their uses. Do not be eccentric and carry too much. Poorly executed captures are harmful.
- The force shall evacuate and retreat at 23:00 hours.
- Before leaving, set watch fires to be left burning at all positions. Paper banners shall be left standing.
- Be prepared for swift infiltration by the mountain enemy sentries and spies on the skirmish line. One hundred strong men shall remain after the allies leave the mountain. If the enemy is patient, do not be rash and attack.
- Having no need for a strong force, I shall lead a small cavalry force of the following twelve men from the central troops.

      Chisaka Naizen
      Ichikawa Shuzen
      Wada Hyoubu
      Uno Samasuke
      Okuni Heima
      Wada Kihei
      Imokawa Heidayu
      Nagai Genshiro

Iwai Toshiro
Takemata Choshichi
Kiyono Kokusho
Inaba Hikoroku

Kenshin jotted down the above in a note. He also gave verbal instructions to runners to inform even the units at the foot of the mountain.

"The order was given to the commanders to promptly return home tomorrow. So have them immediately prepare the loads and tie them to the horses. It is hard to foresee giving the command to depart before 23:00 hours unless there is an emergency. Whatever the time, be ready to set off right away. If cut off by the enemy along the way, the best plan is to head to Zenkoji."

Of course, this declaration came after thorough preparation without leaking the subtleties of the strategy among the rank and file of the allies until a short time ago.

At some time on some night, Kaizu Castle of the Koshu force was filled with the spirits of war and killing.

Every last man in the twenty-thousand-strong force wore full gear including sturdy footwear. The force was split into the two divisions of the *Taiki* and the *Taisei* on the broad grounds in the castle enclosure.

Their stomachs filled, the soldiers stopped eating and carried sufficient provisions in their packs. The gun unit set fires with diameters of two-and-a-half-feet. Two small wooden food boxes tied together hung from the hips of each man who also tied two leather bullet cases on the left and right sides of his waistband.

The large division was the long-handled spear unit. They were the backbone, the pride of Koshu, and carried fifteen- and eighteen-feet long-handled spears like a forest. Many elite warriors among the so-called elites on horseback were in this unit.

"This time …" says the man who strives for a great exploit in the approaching war.

"Is something happening?"

"Not yet."

Crowded together and jostling each other, the twenty thousand warriors and warhorses pushed each other and scuffled inside the limited castle enclosure as they waited for the order to advance.

Already armed, Shingen sat on a camp stool in the lookout tower as his allies swayed before his eyes. This night, his fiery eyes glared at the distant Mount Saijo.

At that moment, the lookouts of the Koshu force detected and relayed updates on movements on Mount Saijo.

"I'm guessing the enemy has begun lashing packs to the packhorses. I see signs of the earth moving over there."

"The Echigo force will retreat tomorrow and withdraw to their home country."

"Just as I expected," said Shingen delighted in hitting on their strategy.

50
THE SETTING MOON

THE OVERALL STRATEGY of the Koshu force was an example of the Woodpecker Strategy that splits the entire force in two in order to strike one side of the enemy and to capture or annihilate the other side.

Twelve thousand men in Uesugi's total force of twenty thousand were provided for the Taisei and passed through Tadagoe crossing in the hills at the foot of the mountain and came out at Kiyono to launch a splendid surprise morning attack through a so-called frontal assault.

The remaining eight thousand troops passed through the Hirose crossing, advanced to the plains of Kawanakajima. The inevitable descent of Uesugi's force from Mount Saijo showing signs of defeat and running away was expected. In other words, this strategy was an ambush via an unconventional tactic.

"What time is it?" asked Shingen over and over.

Attendants advised him about the sky, wind direction, temperature, amount of rain, etc. The elderly man with the air of a Confucian scholar always by Shingen's side was Yamamoto Kansuke Nyudo Douki.

"It's around quarter to ten," answered Kansuke Nyudo Douki.

Shingen nodded then asked, "When will the moon set?"

Kansuke answered after asking his adviser.

"The moon will set tonight on September 9 around forty minutes after midnight."

"Then it'll be soon."

"Yes, it will be soon."

"Minbu. Is Baba Minbu here?"

"Yessir. I'm here."

"At midnight, sound the shells. Pound the large drums to go to war."

"Yessir."

"When they leave the castle gate, the twelve thousand troops of the Taisei will leave first. Don't go to fast and end up in squabbles."

Each general already understood, but Shingen was careful.

To while away the time until gathering here, a sudden change came with the advance of the night's weather. During the evening, slivers of moonlight slipped between sporadic rain clouds, then unnoticed, the clouds in the sky were swept to the side and the heavenly body of an expansive starfield appeared. When preparing for a fight whether a standard attack or an unconventional attack, a moonlit night is always despised.

However, it was midnight.

"Drum unit! Beat the drums!"

At the same time Baba Minbu shouted the signal, the three conch-shell trumpeters who stood facing the three sides of the lookout tower touched the conch shells to their lips, filled their lungs, and blew.

Long. Short. Long again.

On the grounds of the castle filled with footsteps, the echoes of the clattering tassets on their armor and the clip-clopping of horses' hooves could be heard flowing out like a startling wave.

"Excuse me," said Yamamoto Nyudo Douki who was the first to stand.

"With your permission ..."

One after the other Obu Heibu, Kasuga Danjo, Baba Nobuhara, Sanada Yukitaka, Oyamada Bitchu-no-kami, Amari Saemon, Aiki Ichibei, and Obata Yamashiro-no-kami addressed Shingen and stood to leave his presence.

These generals all belonged to the standard assault unit on Mount Saijo and stationed near the hilly crossing at the foot of the mountain.

Shingen himself stood at Kaizu for a short time after watching the departure of the first twelve thousand troops from the castle. He would command the eight thousand in the unconventional attack platoon and take an entirely different route, cross at Hirose, and aim for Hachimanbara. The distance was not very far, but twelve thousand soldiers and horses followed by eight thousand more formed into ranks and leaving the castle gate took a long time. The battle formation coalesced at Hachimanbara before the target Kawanakajima around half past three as dawn approached.

As soon as Shingen arrived, he pointed and said, "Headquarters will be inside the compound of Hachiman Shrine," then ordered, "Rake the ground, build earthen bulwarks, and dig trenches at critical positions."

As the engineers began their industrious work on the black earth, the curtain enclosure of Shingen's headquarters was stretched around the grounds of Hachiman Shrine. The banner of the descendant and the banner of the deity Suwa had already shaken off blood and flapped in the wind. Beginning with the twelve generals in the field headquarters and the more than one hundred hatamoto warriors on horseback, if the eyebrows of the eight thousand officers and men were dampened by the fog, and their straw sandals and leggings were covered by mist from the grass, their easily aroused energy was certainly tapped down by *tanden* meditation focusing just below the navel.

This morning's thick fog was remarkable perhaps the fault of rain showers the previous evening. The dense fog made judging the shortest of distances impossible. And as much as the light rain falling from the banner and battle standard raised beside the commander on horseback differed little from the moisture falling off a helmet's visor, the dripping never ceased.

51
ABANDONED BONFIRES

THE ADVANCE OF the standard attack platoon via a detour through the mountain crossing was a strenuous march.

The road from Saijo rose up. The Tadagoe crossing split and the road narrowed.

While waiting for the moon to set, their hidden *shinobi* pine torches were fairly compact but singed the sky too much with their flames. They feared enemy scouts would smell them.

The mountain was small but had steep paths and valleys. The soldiers and horses were drenched with sweat when they emerged at the Kiyono plain. Needless to say, moving a short distance took time, and the men and horses worked so hard they labored to breathe like the battle just ended.

"This fog is thick …"

"It's divine protection. The enemy won't detect us until we're almost on top of them."

The two units of Amari and Sanada split off to go down different paths.

This was for a surprise attack from above the watchtower to the rear gate of Mount Saijo.

At that time, the night was starting to brighten, and September 10 had come.

The first battle cry of this huge battle rose at daybreak from this attack position.

It was a surprise attack at dawn.

The attack conch shells, bells, and drums sounded. Heaven and Earth shook in unison as the sounds rushed up Mount Saijo from the side and the front.

The voices of twelve thousand warriors made Heaven and Earth tremble.

Small birds rose like ashes all around. The trees on the entire mountain shuddered. Their leaves dropped like rain within the swirling thick fog.

"Wha … what?"

"What the hell?"

"An army of the air."

"Those are paper banners."

Here and there, the same shouts of dismay and shock could be heard. The human figures they came with tremendous force to battle were no longer on this mountain. They were angered by the paper banners dampened by fog and indignant at the still-burning abandoned bonfires.

"We've been outmaneuvered!"

Many legs of warriors wearing straw sandals kicked out and stomped on the camouflaged encampment across the mountain. They admonished each other.

"Be on guard."

"The enemy may show himself!"

"Too bad. Kenshin already knew about our allies' movements."

Takeda's force was too late.

Kenshin was probably smiling. His force retreated the previous night under the moonlight, quietly, cleanly, skillfully.

The soldiers probably tied shut their horses' mouths, descended the mountain under the moon, and waded across Chikuma River after the moon set. The sheaths on the blade tips of the long-handled spears and the long swords were immersed in the waters of the dark autumn. The snaking line of the entire force crossed to the opposite shore at Komasse.

"Oumi, Oumi!" Kenshin suddenly shouted and stopped his horse before the swift currents. "Come here," he said beckoning Amakasu Oumi-no-kami from the rear ranks to his side. Kenshin leaned over on his saddle to whisper to him.

52
ARTERIES AND VEINS

"SEPARATE THE UNIT over there from the main troops, go ahead upstream about five miles, cross at Junikase, and set up camp near the small forest on the northern shore of the Chikuma."

"Yessir."

"And I think this broad, dark plain and the dry riverbed in a thick fog are all the shadows of the enemy. If you're on the alert and see any scouts hanging around, don't let even one escape."

"Understood."

"The main force of the Koshu force will cross downstream of Hirose and move out to Hachimanbara. The left wing, that is the side of the plains northeast of the locations of their camps, is probably closer to the enemy. While listening carefully for their movements, send messengers one after another each time a change is detected."

"Yessir. I understand your intentions completely."

Amakasu Oumi-no-kami bowed to Kenshin on horseback and left. His intentions meant discovering the formation desired by Kenshin. The short interval until accomplishing that for Kenshin was the final command to the unit surveilling the Koshu force.

Amakasu's platoon of about one thousand troops galloped to the southern shore of Chikuma and rushed to Junikase.

While Kenshin watched from the crossing downstream at Amenomiya, the figures of Amakasu's platoon quickly moving to the small forest and crossing the river formed a white spray and a night fog. Were they men or water? Water or fog? Their movements only recalled phantoms.

"Excellent!"

Kenshin's horse washed its legs splashing across the ripples.

When the river runs dry, it becomes a large streak. When rainfall accumulates in the mountains of the headwaters, numerous water veins are swiftly drawn on this vast basin like arteries and veins on the human body.

53

DARK SKIES

EXCEPT FOR AMAKASU Oumi-no-kami's troops, the entire force crossed with the large unit of packhorses of Naoe Yamato-no-kami at the front. Both horses and men were drenched.

"Shh! ... Keep the horses quiet."

One unruly horse whose muzzle had been removed shook its ears and mane and neighed loudly. As the agitated horse neighed, the commander of the unit sprung to press the horse's head tight against his chest.

Thankfully, the neighing stopped.

The horse calmed down without him having to beg. The advance from this point demanded silence with each step.

Flickering lights scattering red from the soldiers' hips were the lights of fuses. They tried their best to hide them to avoid alerting the enemy, but the enemy may have already smelled them. After spotting the enemy, the fuses were not lit in time.

A row of trees on the left resembled the Hokkoku Kaido Road.

Ahead were the sounds of the waters of the Sai River and the shadows resembling a grove of trees at Tamba Island.

In any case, the fog was thick, and the night was an ink-black darkness. Without a certain goal, Kakizaki Izumi-no-kami at the vanguard advanced while groping for the direction. The entire force of more than twelve thousand warriors, horses, and carts stepped onto Kawanakajima while muffling assorted noises. They marched north to the shore of the Sai River.

"The general army will return home to Echigo" was heard the previous evening in the sweep of the force from Mount Saijo. A large contingent of officers and soldiers believed that and had not the slightest doubt they were going north to cross the Sai River and heading to Zenkoji Temple. The large packhorses at the head, Kakizaki Izumi's unit at the vanguard, the two main units, three arboreal platoons, Shibata's unit, Nagao's unit, and the hatamoto under Kenshin in the central force halted the march in the rear before the waters of the Sai River.

The wild, gleaming river waters could be seen ahead in the gaps among the throng of horses and soldiers. The paper-fringed standard of the large turnip of Kakizaki's unit or the Hinomaru banner and the banner of the central army Bishamon, a guardian god of Buddhism, only howled pointlessly. Time passed but the horses did not advance and warriors did not walk. More than ten thousand shadows of warriors and horses piled up behind them. The huge pitch-black group only swelled in the fog.

"Has the vanguard crossed over?"

"Not yet.... It doesn't seem like it."

"What's happened?"

"Don't know. What? The lord in the central army is surrounded, and a couple of generals are making their way to him."

"A standing council?"

As these whispers were murmured among the foot soldiers unit in the rear, Kenshin faced the entire force and his voice could be heard.

"Except for the small and large packhorses, in order from the vanguard unit, move east to Hachimanbara keeping the Sai River to your left. Detour and advance slowly."

The horses' straw sandals kicked out pebbles. The lines of soldiers went around to the right. Next, a conventional column change was executed while walking and turning around. The clean preparation began to arrange into the battle formation called Three Columns, Four Stages.

The time interval was from four to six in the morning. And the skies were dark.

Because of that darkness and the fog, both the Echigo and Koshu armies went unobserved. At this time, in the area surrounding Hachiman Shrine just before Hachimanbara designated by Kenshin as the site for his camp Takeda's huge army had already spread out in that area. Plenty of ditches had been dug, and earthworks built.

Their distances from each other would later become known, but the vanguards of the two armies were less than three-quarters of a mile apart.

54

A HOUSE

"HEY.... WHAT'S going on?"

Tsuruna lifted her head from the pillow.

Her complexion was pallid, except for her bronze cheeks and neck sunburned during her travels, because illness had confined her to bed for more than twenty days.

"Horses neighing ... those voices ... Something's going on."

She strained to hear but was startled by pain somewhere in her body that made it impossible to rise from the bed.

"Priest! Priest!" she called to the next room.

Here in the middle of Hachimanbara, a house stood surrounded by a thicket of trees. The old-fashioned archway to the Shinto shrine was near the house. The elderly priest lived there with his family.

At dusk twenty days earlier, Tsuruna was felled by a bullet on the shore of the Chikuma River, rescued by men who happened to be cutting horse feed, and carried here to be cared for by this shrine family.

Since then, she had been cared for by the kind elderly priest who treated her wound. Because he was an amateur who removed the lead bullet, her foot was swollen from her instep to the ankle of her left leg. She could not walk ten steps.

"Priest! Ma'am!"

No one replied. She crawled to the adjacent room and cried out, "It's war at last. Battles will be fought nearby. If the children aren't moved somewhere else very soon, they'll be hurt. A hail of bullets and stray arrows will fly into this place.... Ma'am, are you awake?"

Her leg throbbed with pain. When she tried to get up, she couldn't. She crawled to the papered sliding door and opened it.

Then she crawled to the other room.

No one answered. Where did the elderly priest, his daughter, and her child go? The bedroom had become the husk of sloughed-off skin. She was slightly shocked but remained calm. She guessed that the daughter quickly gathered her child, her husband helped the old priest, and they escaped to some unknown place.

"Is the Kofu army or Echigo force camped here?"

She had been left in this house alone. If she felt sad, her face did not look lonely.

The pine tree grove outside howled in the sky. The voices of the falling leaves wrapped around the fog. She recognized the sounds of soldiers' footsteps mingled with the noise of the wind swirling around the house.

The family fled so quickly they left the door open. The veranda storm shutters had been removed, and the kitchen door had been knocked down. All of a sudden, a huge figure appeared near the dark water jar. He made a rattling sound, started to search for a pail, and approached the side of the back well.

He raised the well bucket and ladled water into the pail. The shadow of the armored warrior resembled a giant.

"Ah! Father. Is that you, Father?" shouted Tsuruna.

Gripping the pole of the well bucket, only the warrior's eyes and nose were visible through his helmet with a metal visor and thin gold cheek guards when he turned to look inside the room and stared for a short time at Tsuruna.

55
THE ARMORED PARENT

AS IF HE were deaf and dumb, the warrior did not react. He let go of the well bucket but held onto the ladle and walked forward in silence.

"... Ah!"

She ran down rather tumbled down the veranda.

The pain of the swelling on her leg vanished. She followed the warrior carrying the bucket in one hand and heading down the lane through the thicket of trees.

"You are Fa ... Father, aren't you? You're a Koshu retainer. You are Hajikano Den'emon ..."

"No."

"No, you're not."

"No, no."

"The crest on your armor breastplate is the ginger of the Hajikano clan."

"Ginger is another clan."

"I can't remember anything. It's only been four or five years since I left the Kofu clan. Have I forgotten the clan's crest?"

"Who are you?"

"I'm Tsuruna. Father. From just your eyes and voice, I know I'm your child. Why don't you call me Tsuruna?"

"I don't know."

"Your command was harsh. I was just fourteen and on a pilgrimage to Zenkoji Temple with you Father. Out of nowhere, you gave me the stern orders — You will abandon yourself to benefit Koshu, be loyal to the lord, and find your way to Echigo. I was cared for by kind people and went into service in the house of the hatamoto Kurokawa Osumi on Mount Kasuga.... When we parted, I earnestly obeyed what you said. I sent secret written messages to Kofu describing in endless detail the events in the Uesugi clan, the actions in the castle town, and the rumors circulating in the clan.... But it was useless."

A bullet rang out from somewhere. Its sound waves traveled across the vast field, shook the fog, and penetrated to this thicket of trees.

"Let's go! Where do you think we are?"

Den'emon quickened his pace.

Water from the bucket splashed onto Tsuruna's back. Without looking around, Hajikano Den'emon ran off between the trees like that water was far more important than his daughter.

56
THE REVELATION OF A SECRET

THE LOG RUNNING the length of the cypress roof of the shrine was visible. Hachiman Shrine was an ancient hall of worship. Curtained field enclosures were stretched out at various locations across a fairly broad area with their backs to the south face of the shrine.

Shingen's headquarters were said to be the entire zone reaching the size of a town of two-and-a-half square miles. With so many identical enclosures, the one in which Shingen sat on a camp stool could not be known without searching for the flag emblem or the paper-fringed standard.

"I found freshwater," said Hajikano Den'emon who had passed into one of the enclosures. Shingen was obviously in there.

The camp stool was empty, and Shingen was standing. His entire body was filled with a fighting spirit. The furious motion of his blood since the previous night dried out his mouth. For some time, he frequently asked for a cup of water. Although a common soldier should have been sent on this sort of errand, even a servant became apprehensive when sent for drinking water for the lord. Den'emon went out to search and eventually found and returned with well water.

"Ah, delicious. That was satisfying."

In a gulp, Shingen drank about half of the water in the ladle and returned it to the bucket.

The handle of the ladle banged against the bucket's rim. His large ears sprouting hair stood like it was giving some kind of hint.

"... Well, Den'emon did you hear it?"

"What?"

"It's a strange thing.... I can't explain it."

"If you mean the sound of gunfire, I heard it on the way back."

"No, that was a confused, cowardly sentry in the camp mistakenly firing a shot at Tenkyu Nobushige. No, not that. There were other more numerous, colorless, toneless sounds. What could they have been? The thick fog creates a blinding whiteness, but I keenly sense something approaching from above the camp.... Ah, of course. Those were the movements of horses and soldiers. Bungo! Bungo!"

At the curtain opening, four or five hatamoto and Morozumi Bungo-no-kami, who stood on guard holding a long-handled spear, responded by taking five of six steps out.

"Have the critical trenches been dug? And are the bulwarks finished? Not yet?"

"The foot soldiers are busy in front under the command of Naito and on the flank under Ogasawara."

That voice? Who was panting? Shingen wondered again and for a short time calmed himself but suddenly called to Mochizuki Jinhachiro, the commander of the scouts to ask, "Have the scouts you sent out reported on any signs at the Amenomiya crossing or in the Komori area? Has anyone returned?"

"Just one," replied the slightly ashamed Jinhachiro. He looked at Shingen's face then asked, "Would you like to see him?"

Had Shingen's sensitivity touched on something at that moment? His large eyes looked to the sky as his body jumped from the camp stool. He shouted, "I didn't expect that."

"No messenger has come from the allies who launched an assault on Mount Saijo. You say none of the scouts have returned, but you didn't mention the enemy force of Uesugi coming to this place … What was it?! … What was that sound of legions of men and horses?"

The officers and men in the enclosures heard his words. The echoes of top-tier suits of armor were heard. A rumbling of the Earth seemed to approach the troops gathered into corps. The aura around Shingen shimmered.

"Don't get upset," said an untroubled Shingen. Their feelings were soothed when they looked at his complexion and his large physique. Shingen called out, "Urano Minbu. Minbusaemon. Go out on patrol immediately. No need to bow, go now."

In a rush to return with an answer, half of Minbusaemon's body could be seen high above the camp enclosure as he leaped onto his horse.

By applying the whip, he returned with an answer in no time. He jumped down and soon was kneeling before Shingen to give his report.

"An enemy force is there."

"Is it Uesugi's force?"

"Long columns are on a northern path moving toward the Sai River."

"Has his vanguard crossed the Sai yet?"

"They're turning right from that area and gradually forming a large crescent shape. At their pace, even if the battle begins, they realize they will not arrive very quickly? …" said Urano Minbusaemon with a tinge of doubt as he looked into Shingen's eyes. Shingen read his mind from the uncertainty in his eyes and his sober nod.

The scout's report also showed the way. The enemy's fighting spirit was strained. They are driven by panic and confusion. And the enemy's strengths, as a rule, were not spoken of without reason. If the truth were not spoken, the decisions of the commanders would be wrong. There are what the eyes convey and possibly the rumors from mouths deliberately falsifying what surrounds the lord. In essence, that can be said to be quick wit at the spur of the moment.

57

THE SPINNING WHEEL

GOOD GOD! HAD Kenshin descended the mountain?

Surprise gripped Shingen, but his brow didn't move.

However, his intuition gave him an instant understanding of the magnitude of the situation.

"…"

After listening to Usano Minbusaemon's report, his big eyes glared behind his eyelids. The rush of air escaping his nostrils was audible. The iron war fan in Shingen's right hand left his knees.

"As a precaution, Muroga Nyudo, go out on patrol one more time. How does a general like Kenshin abandon a camp occupied for over twenty days and set about to withdraw to his country without a fight? Also, he crossed the Chikuma before night and passed the night near here, so this cannot be understood as a simple withdrawal. Minbu, I think you're mistaken. Quickly go again and assess the state of Kenshin's preparations," ordered Shingen pointing at the face of a man in the corner.

"Yessir. I'm off."

Muroga Nyudo was a provincial samurai and familiar with the geography of this region. He jumped onto the horse, applied his whip, and galloped away. Next, Shingen called Hara Masatane and Yamamoto Kansuke Nyudo Douki, and commanded the pair to approach his camp stool and hurriedly whispered something to them.

Around that time, the faint light of dawn was visible on their faces. The night began to brighten. However, no one could tell the color of another's eyes in the deep morning fog. Not only was vision blocked by this fog, but even sounds could not slip through. The neighs of the allies' horses were easily muffled and unheard.

Shingen calculated that was sufficient. Meticulous knowledge of ordinary military strategy was useful to the five sense organs to prevent the creation of

EIJI YOSHIKAWA

errors from the general notions of ordinary vision and hearing. Nevertheless, the errors he expected in the estimate of the distance to the enemy would soon be obvious.

"I saw them," shouted the returning Muroga Nyudo. The situation became more urgent than an emergency. In a short time, he bowed and gave a detailed report.

"The entire Echigo force saw the allies on the right and repeatedly put pressure on the solid columns to go to the Sai River while keeping an eye on this place. In fact, while drawing a large eddy like a whirlpool across Hachimanbara, they are gradually shrinking the separation from our force."

As soon as he heard this, Shingen preened like an eagle hitting its wings, jumped up and said, "So that's what he's up to. That's the Spinning Wheel."

"In that case, Masatane, as Kansuke Nyudo just said, the allies are difficult to support with this level of preparation because of the enemy's readiness and the pressure being applied by a military maneuver. Quickly change the battle formation of the military units at various locations following Kansuke's orders."

58
YES OR NO

THE FIRST STAGE of the war on that day in Kawanakajima began from contact with Uesugi's Spinning Wheel. No, the beginning was not the military formation of the Spinning Wheel but in ancient times with the problem of boisterous disputes between military clans.

However, Uesugi Kenshin expected war. His meticulous plan designed for direct and sudden contact with the central axis of the enemy.

In the end, he was unable to carry out this plan because he could not divide Shingen's central force with an opposing force required to be a fixed distance from normally hardened positions.

Fortunately, the thick fog made the direction of the entire force seem to be toward the Sai River and retreating homeward. The truth was the soldiers were circling a huge wheel and approaching the front of Shingen's force like a typhoon moving parallel. From the perspective of his resolve, this was called a war strategy but was a natural plan and rational.

An advocate of the opposing view would say, "Today, at the beginning of the war, the whereabouts of Kenshin and Shingen are not precisely known. Because the twenty-thousand-strong Koshu army split in two when they left Kaizu, one passed through the mountains to launch a surprise attack on Mount Saijo. A portion of them crossed at Hirose and came out at Hachimanbara. Therefore, Kenshin's keen insight is unable to discern whether Shingen and the unit directly under his command are in the ambush corps in the hills or in the field operations standby corps. Nevertheless, in a battle formation that risks death like the Spinning Wheel, there is no reason to recklessly instigate a challenge to the enemy."

Although this looks like a reason, only Kenshin's impact is seen, and the thoughts in his mind are missing. Before leaving Mount Saijo, the reconnaissance team he sent out provided one report after another every hour while crossing the river in the march from there. Without a doubt, the absence of solid proof about Shingen's presence in any of his camps in the reports coming in one after another suggested Kenshin did not receive sufficient data to make that determination.

Furthermore, following the written words of the patriarch of the Uesugi clan, Kenshin ordered the two hatamoto Yamayoshi Genban and Suga Tajima, in particular, to carry out deep surveillance to accurately pinpoint his objective after coming to this plain.

They entered the patrol zone of the Koshu force.

Deep surveillance was not an ordinary patrol but the task of spying deep inside enemy territory to search at risk to their lives and demanded the skill of invisibility.

The fog was thick on Heaven and Earth at dawn. In the haze among the figures of men and the curtain enclosures of the allies, predictions were not made about the positions of men who weren't allies and resembled field mice lurking around.

The preparation at Shingen's location in the central force concealed the banner of the grandson, the most emblematic of the Koshu army; the Dharma flag; the religious flag of Suwa Myojin Shrine; and the flower-shaped crest flag. They weren't so careless as to give away Shingen's location to the enemy in a glance.

59
THE CENTIPEDE BANNERS

EXCUSE THIS DIGRESSION about a matter from long ago. When Oda Nobunaga attacked the central army of Imagawa Yoshimoto at Okehazama, he was uncertain about Yoshimoto's whereabouts until he raided his camp. While searching for him, he came across a beautifully lacquered palanquin. For the first time, Nobunaga's subordinates gained the conviction to strengthen their courage to compete for success.

In addition, Shingen, an uncommonly cautious man, was said to have eight kagemusha, decoy warriors, but why. Despite having seen the life in the camps of Tokugawa Ieyasu and Oda Nobunaga, there were many instances of a proxy being installed at the troop headquarters while the man himself took the initiative to secretly join the front line to take direct command. Somehow, Shingen didn't understand the purpose of the eight permanent kagemusha and may have viewed the frequent use of proxies to be a grave error.

Some doubted the effect of the Spinning Wheel battle formation. However, based on Yamaga Sokou's writings on military strategy, the following was a consideration.

> The Spinning Wheel sets out for the enemy's preparations and has advantages if used in three and four stages. This is said to be for a small force. If used on a large force, ten or eleven stages face the enemy, and there is no advantage.

The value of the wheel-shaped battle formation was adequately recognized but emphasized a dependence on the rival's preparation. In opposition to this theory, Ogyu Sorai of the same generation opposed the Spinning Wheel. Sorai strongly argued there was no reason for Kenshin to use the Spinning Wheel because Takeda's formation at the time was the serious configuration of the so-called Twelve Layers of Fish Scales.

However, ever-present change is the reality of military formations. The essence of a military formation is to always undergo rapid change. Persistent use of the Crane's Wing, the Serpentine, or the Bird Cloud battle formation produces dead formations not living ones.

The Spinning Wheel! thought Shingen in a flash of intuition. He hurried to give orders to Hara Hayanosho and the allied units. Needless to say, the response of *change* was the immediate order.

In this case, the reason for the slight confusion on Shingen's face was until this moment Shingen held this conviction, I will get the jump on Echigo's force. He ordered a surprise attack unit to head to Mount Saijo. The ambush unit will take up positions here and wait for the collapse of the enemy. The entire purpose was to observe the entire situation as in a game of shogi in order to seize every initiative.

However, his position was reversed.

Without a doubt, Kenshin would continue to drive forward. Just before this situation occurred, the allies' positions needed to be changed. In other words, Shingen had been outmaneuvered.

The junior warrior Kenshin stumped Shingen with his splendid move in a strategy of divine wisdom and technique. In human terms, Shingen, who exhibited the discretion of a veteran and faith in final victory, was only enraged by "little Kenshin's behavior." This filled Shingen with the spirit of "I will teach him a lesson."

60
THE LONG VIEW

"THE LORD'S ORDER is to change the battle formation."

"Change the formation."

Several courier guards on horseback with the centipede banners of Takeda inserted behind their backs galloped to the units of the allies to report like a spreading fire to the positions.

"In Lord Yamagata's writing, the order is to drive forward into the midst of the advance guard and stand with the banners of white Chinese bellflowers as the sign."

"The men of Takeda Tenkyu Nobushige and Anayama Genba in the forces on the left will see the white bellflowers of Lord Yamagata."

"Murozumi Bungo and Naito Shuri Masatoyo are in the forces on the right."

"Lord Shingen and the hatamoto are in the center."

"Next, Hara Hayato and Takeda Shoyoken will prepare on the left flank."

"Takeda Taro Yoshinobu and Mochizuki Jinhachiro will make preparations on the right flank. And the rear guard will be Atobe Ohinosuke, Imafuku Joukansai, and Asari Shikibushouyu …"

With speed, booming voices, and urgency, the messengers of Takeda's Centipede unit galloped around to pass on these orders. Yamagata Saburobei's company at the vanguard and other units moved out like a cloud materializing in the valley, but they were already too late.

The flowing motion of Kenshin's amazing Spinning Wheel formation drew closer and was right before their eyes.

That technique of closing in on the enemy was not a rapid frontal assault. The links in a huge iron chain closed in while endlessly circling round and round. The location of the sharp angle of the combat force is where it hurls itself against the advance guard of the enemy.

Now, one end seems to come into contact somewhere with another end.

135

Still, Takeda revamped the entire battle formation before a foothold was established.

Naturally, signs of confusion appeared in the camp.

Shingen probably thought about the backflow of blood here. Perhaps, the sounds of the large drums suddenly rang in succession through brave tones because of the proximity to his curtained enclosure.

However, combat was the key.

The sounds of the large taiko drums were not the start of a reckless offense.

"Messenger! Messenger!" called out a nearby hatamoto. Yamamoto Donyu and Hara Hayato returned immediately to his respective station and disappeared from this place.

"Yessir! You called."

Several men bearing the centipede banner came running. Their eyes, lips, and complexions were not normal.

"More orders! The left and right units in the vanguard will hold their posts and not leave the camp without a purpose for even a moment. A fierce attack by the enemy will be defended to the death at those positions. Contact the commander at each position immediately."

When orders were received again from headquarters, each messenger waved the centipede banner on his back as he pleased and left running.

He used drums, and the other side deliberately used chimes.

In any case, the mutual enemies saw each other. The hairs over their whole bodies stood on end at their eyes, their ears, and the tips of their toes.

At some unknown time, the sun rose in the sky.

When the position of the sun was examined, the time was exactly seven in the morning. The fog had not yet burned off, but a clear band cut through the milky white fog and turbulence rose and fell like clouds of steam and hung at places of a thin film. Needless to say, the Sai and Chikuma Rivers from the surface of Kawanakajima were embossed in a bright haze to the far-off Myoko and Kurohime mountain chain.

"They're close. They're closing in."

"Two-hundred forty to three hundred feet."

"No, only one hundred eighty feet."

The crawling, meandering line furthest in front of the vanguard was the rifle squad of the small unit under the command of Yamagata Saburobei.

"… not yet. Not yet."

He loaded the ammunition. Then from the shadows of the small basin, he assessed the distance while aiming at the enemy and effortlessly took a shot.

"Still another one hundred twenty feet. Get closer."

That voice coming from behind was probably the group commander.

Still aiming, the gunners had been prepared for a long time.

If the least bit negligent during that time, the flint went out in the damp fog on the autumn grass, and the ammunition got wet.

"Not yet?"

"I can't."

The range of rifles at that time was no more than one hundred eighty feet. The best bullets delivered would bounce off the body armor and the tassets. Three light slugs or heavier lead bullets weighing one-half to one ounce were finally shot. The rifle could not be used again without cleaning the scorched parts of the barrel or the cartridge.

This troublesome machine was a state-of-the-art weapon and debuted on the battlefield a few years earlier. The wealthy Koshu force and the culturally sensitive Kenshin eventually had only one hundred twenty or one hundred thirty guns in their entire armies.

Thus, a single shot held the prospect of "the enemy will not be shot."

The preferred target was an important man so "if the enemy falls, he will be a general."

Hopes could certainly be achieved through conventional bows. More than the lead archer, the lead gunner apologized to the lord for his lack of success at the start of the war. The muzzles of just twenty or thirty men were in their hands but had a substantial effect on the military nature of the entire force.

The sounds of the footsteps, even those of the enemy, soon echoed in their ears.

The driving revolving motion was not only the figures in Uesugi's force. The grayness of the fog swirled with frightening power. Each time sunlight penetrated, a multitude of some object glinted in the light behind the fog.

The long-handled spear unit of the Uesugi clan was famous. The brave warriors held a sharp weapon like the pattern affixed to a long sword. As he thought this, the revolving line left the night fog like a rapid current before his eyes, and another unit appeared instantly. One column of a fence of spears approached on foot like a sudden squall.

The mouth of the lead gunner opened and released a full-throated voice.

"Shoot!"

Bang! Bang!

The reports of the guns echoed unevenly. The dampness had affected the ammunition. Five or six of the twenty guns did not fire.

But the sharp echoes and the smell of the rising gun smoke were enough to agitate the blood of the Koshu warriors. Enemy and ally were separated by one hundred fifty to sixty feet. A lone battle cry rose and shook the morning on Heaven and Earth.

61
LIFE ON A KILLING FIELD

AS THE IMPRESSIVE front line of the enemy put their madness on full view in their steady push forward in clusters, a thunderous war cry came from one of the lines. It was answered by a battle cry from the other side.

As more shouts and calls rose, both sides walked step by step into the space between them. This situation in the camp being approached did not easily reveal the next development. One step forward was accompanied by a shout. A crawl forward by half a step also came with a shout.

Rather than approaching the enemy on foot, voices as powerful as possible approached. The voices doing this the right way turned into rasps.

When courage was aroused at the start of the war, lifting only voices was not enough. Ferocious drums rang out behind the front ranks. There was also a technique to striking the drums. It is said that if the drummer did not have the spirit found in devotion to prayers in Heaven and Earth or strike with frantic effort, the footsteps of allied warriors cannot walk toward the enemy and push them aside.

In this case, they did not look like brave warriors as if everyone flinched at the start of the war. When veterans stepped on and faced many battlefields, they often experienced the moment of the first sighting of the shadows of the enemy and making the first push toward the camp. However, every last one of the brave warriors was, in fact, terrified.

This is a man far in the future, but in an old book relating an account told by Miyake Gunbei of the Togun-ryu school of swordsmanship, the recollections of the soldiers explained the terror of this glimpse on the battlefield.

"The enemy of a fence of spears and the ally of a fence of spears edged forward with their legs packed together. Shouts went back and forth several tens of times. Eventually, drums were no longer heard. Our voices were no longer distinguishable as human, and we were blind. When the hands holding spears stiffened, all tranquility vanished, and, in an instant, Heaven and Earth were experienced as pitch black, then the faces of the enemy flashed into view. No one took one step out of the enemy line. The allies lined up the tips of their spears. Not one man ran out. When this place is the abyss or a void, legs trembled and hearts darkened from the instant the first unknown man among the swarming enemy pushed forward alone and a man frantically hurled his body at him. But at first, we forget and, encouraged by that courageous man, one after the other ran into the enemy. Thus, the warrior performing the great deed of being the first to run out cannot be captured by a careless enemy. Adept military men are not easily made and are men of ordinary courage. All of them are nearly identical on the battlefield no matter how many times they've stepped onto one. We remember the difficulty in suppressing our trembling bodies only at the beginning."

A warrior like Gunbei spoke like this. He recounted this story later to those who asked about his experience when he borrowed the camp of the Matsudaira clan at the Siege of Osaka in the summer and winter and engaged in a courageous fight. Perhaps, he was not speaking only about himself or the Siege of Osaka and this occurred at the start of any battle?

62
AMPUTATION

THE CLOSE COMBAT at Kawanakajima had already been slightly affected by firearms. Naturally, military units further out front tended to be set up during the battle formation.

In general, the four-stage arrangement had the common sense to place the gun regiment in front, followed by the archery regiment, the long-handled spear regiment, and the warriors.

Usually, gun units began shooting when seven hundred to one hundred feet from the enemy.

Bullets could not cross that distance, but the warriors' voices hit the objective of raising spirits like the drums.

When the distance shrunk to two hundred forty to three hundred feet, the bullets reached the enemy and shooting intensified on both sides.

Because loading bullets and cleaning guns took time, the technique used three rows in three shifts. The men in front took a shot then retreated to the back. Then the men in the next row waited for the loaded guns then moved forward, shot, and retreated to the back.

When they pushed within one hundred eighty feet, the archery unit rained down arrows.

By moving forward another sixty feet and gathering together between forty-two feet and thirty feet, for the first time, the long-handled spear unit or the short spear unit began their attack that turned into hand-to-hand combat. At this time, when the emergency conch shell or the drum sounded, determined foot soldiers and samurai plunged into the enemy to engage in two-handed tactics. Whether holding a long sword, a spear, a tool, or unarmed, regardless of the military technique, they plunged into the melee to win and crush the enemy.

At the start of the war at Kawanakajima on the morning of September 10, this constant rule of war had changed drastically.

The reason was the guess on the Koshu side that the enemy was approaching in the Spinning Wheel formation and pushed on a stronghold more severely than the established rule. For a long time, Kenshin expected to win this time and prepared an uncommon strategy. With his tactic of amputation to cut off the enemy to fight, his assertion to various generals and hatamoto surrounding him was that the winner or loser would not be swiftly decided.

The decisive battle of amputation means the two hands are gone. The four-stage preparation is not the beginning of the war. The objective was an all-out, desperate fight to enter the decisive battle right after the war starts.

Standing at the vanguard was the unit of Kakizaki Izumi-no-kami.

The paper-fringed standard bearing the large turnip was rumpled in the surprise attack. Honjo Kozen-no-kami, Yamayoshi Magojiro, Irobe Shuri, and Yasuda Jibu began shouting from the left and right.

The leader Kenshin should have been surprised by two battle positions opening up near Kakizaki's unit.

If the ally in front came into contact with the enemy and splintered, Kenshin's nearby position would be exposed to the enemy. This was not said to be daring.

Shingen was unable to imagine this coming to pass. The combined wisdom of generals like Yamamoto Kansuke and Hara Hayato was unable to make this deduction. According to form, the Koshu force opened fire with guns on the circling force of the enemy from the rifle unit spread over the front line at important positions. From Uesugi's side, however, as soon as the alarm bells rang and the battle cries poured out, General Kenshin himself shouted, "Amputate. Do not step back. Men in back, step forward!"

Before his mount, the banners with the kanji character for dragon written on a red background hung way up high. Under the loud cries of "Go! Go!" shouts encouraged the men to break the poles, to rip up the banners, and to strike.

The flag with the flowing dragon character was the flag of desperate courage called the Flag of the Charge in the Uesugi clan. When this flag was waved, the entire army under the flag immediately pledged nothing other than to die. That is, they collided with pressure from the enemy. If a warrior flinched and took one step back or retreated half a step, he would not be able to show his face again as a samurai among the people. That was the spirit of honor in the Uesugi clan. This thought of the warrior was that shame is a disgrace.

63
FAREWELL

THEY RAN TOWARD death.

No, they leaped to capture death.

That was not enough. What would be enough?

In an instant, they risked their lives to infiltrate the enemy like a wave of bare swords. This cannot be compared to any other phenomenon of living beings on Earth. It was magnificent, superb, heart-rending, and exhilarating. No words can describe this. If there is greater meaning, it ends here in the beauty of the instant of the culmination of a man's life work.

Everyone from the unit commanders on down among Kakizaki Izumi-no-kami's troops on Uesugi's side rushed in the fastest. The foot soldiers and the samurai lay face down with their helmets on, oblivious to bullets and arrows, war cries rose, a stampede, then the collision.

The unit in the Koshu force under the banner of Yamagata Saburobei Masakage executed the amputation maneuver.

"Dammit! Nozoe! Send the archers and gunners to the back. Long spears, forward! ... Forward now!"

Under the banner of white bellflowers, Sanburobei Masakage leaped up.

Nozoe Magohachi shouted this order to the front line, but the allies had already fallen into confusion.

The outbreak of war took them by surprise. If guns were shot first, while they still believed the enemy would come for now with guns, their powerful enemy had already woven themselves among the allies.

"I'm Odai Kisuke of the Uesugi clan."

"I'm called Somoya Gonnosuke by the people of Mount Kasuga."

"I'm Koshi Samanojo. Watch these hand movements of the Echigo warriors."

The voices heard on the right were also the enemy. Yamagata Masakage's shout of "Dammit!" was too late. Uesugi's soldiers rapidly scattered over the entire encampment like a flood of water gushing in through the ripped bottom of a boat. Here and there, the sun reddened by blood leaked in through breaks in the fog onto the deep crimson of many soldiers cruelly transformed into corpses.

A young Koshu general standing on a small hill like a mound in the field saw the war begin. He was Shingen's younger brother Takeda Tenkyu Nobushige.

With a force of only eight hundred, he was positioned much further to the left than the ally Yamagata.

"What? This Uesugi fighting spirit is not ordinary. I've never once seen an enemy whose fighting was chilling from the start of a war. Today will probably be a hard fight where even a Takeda who does not know defeat will barely escape death," said Tenkyu then prodded his horse with the whip and mumbled, "Well, I will also remember today as a day of death."

He considered rushing to the enemy but instead went down to the front of the encampment of his older brother Shingen, opened the curtain, and immediately stood before Shingen.

He reported on the urgency of the situation, and the precarious siting of the ally's camp in the worst possible position. Nobushige urged his brother not to waver.

"Seriously consider thoughts of good luck to be good luck. It's no exaggeration to say the Takeda clan is in crisis."

Shingen asked with perfect composure, "Tenkyu? Why are you here?"

Nobushige's eyes blurred with tears as he said, "I will leave this world."

Rather than a bow, when Nobushige looked down to hide his tears, Shingen frowned and shouted, "You still have blood relatives on this battlefield. Do you remember that somewhere in your heart? And there are twenty thousand valuable warriors with me. I'm not fretting over the presence of my younger brother. Your emotions are useless. You're getting in the way of this camp's work. Go now."

"I failed. Forgive me," said Tenkyu wiping away tears. He took off on his horse from his brother's camp.

"Nobushige, don't blame yourself," a voice shouted from behind. When he turned to look, it was the vanguard Yamamoto Kansuke Douki.

"Oh, Douki?"

"It's quickly looking like a melee. Unexpectedly, the one who commands you is connected to the unending life. For many years, I've received your great favor. I also know that today is the path to enlightenment, the day to say good-bye forever. I pray for good fortune in war for you."

This encampment was filled with an aura of dread of the rapid breaking through of the front stockade, scattered corpses of allies and enemies, broken spears, and trampled banner holders.

"I will follow one of the path to enlightenment or the road to the hereafter. Anyway, did the enemy send you running to my camp?"

Tenkyu turned to answer, "No, like you Yamamoto Douki, I am not easily defeated. Remember that time we were nearly destroyed by enemy soldiers under the command of Honjo Kozen and Kakizaki Izumi but desperately pushed them back. We took advantage of the enemy falling back and used all our strength to provide support after the collapse of our vanguard troops under Yamagata Masakage."

"... Ah, was that a vortex of men similar to a distant tide?"

"If you hold out, a win by the allies is certain. Last night, ten thousand allies rushed here to launch a sneak attack on Mount Saijo. If you hold out, the winning army today will be our Koshu force ..."

As he spoke, a single command was shouted from behind then the rider galloped off, "Strategist! The preparations on the right flank of Yamagata's troops and the two units of Naito and Morozumi were leveled by an onslaught by Shibata Naganori-no-kami and other enemy soldiers. A command soon came from the top to immediately assist them. Hurry!"

"What? The right flank, too?" asked the senior strategist, who was already past sixty years old then abruptly used his spear as a cane like a man in his prime to stand.

He staggered five or six steps, turned toward Tenkyu again, and said, "Good-bye."

Tenkyu saw him off with a pained look in his eyes. Douki Nyudo's body already bore several spear and bullet wounds. However, he wasn't the least bit daunted. What had he shouted in a strained voice from inside the cloud of combat dust?

64
THE FLOWING HEAD

THAT DAY, TENKYU Nobushige wore armor with white silk and leather braided cords but did not wear a horned-beetle helmet set on his pig head. He carried a long spear under his arm and straddled a black Kai steed. His helmet hung off his back. He smoothed back his rumpled hair with the headband to stanch blood and bravely took command. What was he thinking?

"Gennojo, Gennojo," Nobushige called to the samurai Kasuga Gennojo beside his horse, "This is a memento of my father Nobutora. The theft of this hood with his calligraphy by an enemy would be a stain on my name far into the future. Please keep this and pass it on to my son Nobutoyo."

Nobushige pulled a bluish-purple hood off his back and tossed it to him.

Gennojo hurried to pick it up and said, "Are you ordering me to keep this, return to Kofu alive, and pass it to the young lord? Excuse me for saying, but please give this order to another. At this place, today, I will not retreat one step," he yelled back, rather shrieked or cried, to his lord on horseback.

Tenkyu showed his anger and left with a dismissive comment.

"That order is for you and no other. Return to Kofu immediately."

He gave his abrupt order and plunged into the melee.

The comrades Nojiri Yasuke, Sekikawa Judayu, Kashiwa Kurodo, and Kumasaka Daigo among the Echigo warriors spotted him.

"There's Tenkyu. Shingen's younger brother," said one when he saw Tenkyu and abandoned his companions.

"He's mine," said another and hurtled toward him.

"To get his head would be an honor for a military family and a satisfying kill at the same time."

They stood to block and chase him, doggedly pursuing him to the end.

Tenkyu took his spear, unsheathed his battle sword and cut Kumasaka Daigo.

"Amazing. My turn," said Sekikawa Judayu and extended his spear at an incline. His spear surprised Tenkyu and grazed the front of his head.

"Aaaugh!"

He pulled back with all his might and somersaulted forward over the horse's head. Nojiri and Kashiwa fought him. When they tried to cut off his head, dozens of men under Tenkyu charged in as one but lost sight of Tenkyu in the chaos.

"He got away!"

When they realized that, Tenkyu whipped his horse and retreated to the Chikuma River. He hadn't reached the river when one Echigo warrior took a shot. Tenkyu fell into the river with a splash.

A large force of Echigo warriors galloped into the river, sloshed around and kicked the white-crested waves to raise Tenkyu's head.

Tenkyu's body bobbed up and down in the current. A vassal Umetsuya Munemitsu of Uesugi's general Usami Suruga-no-kami caught the body in his arms. The river instantly turned blood red. He waded through the river again to carry out the severed head under his arm.

But the moment Munemitsu took one step onto shore from the water, Higuchi Saburobei and Yokota Mondo, servants of Tenkyu's family, shouted, "Hand over the head," and stabbed him.

Umetsuya Munemitsu swept his long sword sideways at one and struck down the other. He ran toward his allies while shouting. Perhaps he shouted, "The vassal Umetsuya Munemitsu of Usami Suruga-no-kami shot the head of Shingen's younger brother, Samanosuke Tenkyu Nobushige."

Whatever he was shouting could not be heard among the gasps, the agitation, and many fantastic sounds.

A soldier following close behind, even going as far as Uesugi's side, suddenly slashed Umetsuya Munemitsu's shoulder at a slant killing him and left him lying face down. As soon as the soldier snatched Lord Tenkyu's head from Munemitsu's hand, his face was moistened by tears, and he ran back to Takeda's camp. Although this was determined after the war, that soldier was a young man who Tenkyu favored for some time. He was a low-ranking page called Yamadera Myonosuke.

65
THE HOWLING PLAIN

ONE KOSHU GENERAL named Morozumi Bungo-no-kami suffered from loose bowels that began the previous day. Unable to stand the misery, from time to time, he gave orders while lying on his shield. Now, he cast off the pain of his illness to take up his shield to hold back the enemy.

The attacking Uesugi force was the sharp point of Kakizaki Izumi's troops that punched through the center of the Koshu army.

"Connect to the support of the rank-and-file soldiers. At full speed run past camps two and three and head to the forest at Hachiman. Shingen's headquarters are there," said the voice of the unknown enemy general nearly drowned out by shouts and screams.

Morozumi Bungo-no-kami was frightening. Without trying to gain a useless win in fighting the advance guard, the enemy seemed to zealously target only Shingen's camp.

"They intend to level this place."

When Shingen looked around, his subordinates were fighting desperate battles everywhere. The men engaged in spear-to-spear combat quickly flung away broken spears and disappeared into a mist of blood with their battle swords raised high.

Horses exposed to the deep-red sun ran wildly among them. Men fell from their horses, others were trampled, while others clung to the stirrups as they dragged the enemy off his horse. The men weren't killed on the saddle, instead, they were stabbed and killed by the enemy below and experienced a cruel death in battle.

Or they captured and grappled with the enemy. Grass, dirt, and blood mixed together. A pair desperately struggled until one finally hit the ground and his head was lifted high. A new rival immediately appeared to avenge his fallen comrade-in-arms. In no time, one life after another was unsparingly tossed away. The corpses were stacked into a mountain.

The dew on the leaves and the grasses dried up over the extent of the plain. Instead of the fog clearing away, the plain was shrouded by the dust kicked up by horses and a mist of blood.

Surrounded by human screams that were beyond description, twanging strings, gunshots, horses neighing, and the accompanying rumbling earth, the Uesugi singing in victory, "Tenkyu Nobushige was killed," and one after the other sad voices of the allies saying, "Lord Nobushige died in battle," could be heard by the ears of Morozumi Bungo.

66
THE DEATH IN BATTLE
OF MOROZUMI BUNGO

SOMEHOW BEFORE THAT day, words of foreboding about those who would be slain were divulged.

"On this morning, it was said again and again that today's battle will be the place where Tenkyu will die. The lord's younger brother ..."

At this moment, signs of defeat of Takeda were ubiquitous.

"I will go with him," said Morozumi Bungo who was no bystander and hastened death by inviting one enemy after another.

Driven back by this force, Kakizaki Izumi's unit escaped once, but Shibata Naganori-no-kami's troops, another Uesugi ally, launched an attack on the flank of Morozumi's unit.

Kakizaki's unit turned back. Naturally, the attack converged from both sides, and Bungo-no-kami lost the hard fight.

"I see a famous samurai. I am the Shibata vassal Matsumura Shin'emon. Give me your head."

A man shouted his name as he ran up to Bungo-no-kami from behind.

He turned to see an infantry soldier carrying a spear by its long oak shaft.

He shouted, "Intruder!" turned his horse's head, dropped the stirrups, and swung down his sword from above his head. At the same time, Shin'emon's spear struck the neck of his rival's horse. Bungo fell head over heels off his saddle.

"He's dead. He's dead. This is the head of Takeda's samurai General Morozumi Bungo."

Matsumura Shin'emon danced as he raised the severed head to show both allies and enemies, but the vassals of Bungo-no-kami, Ishiguro Gorobei, Yamadera Toemon, and Hirose Gozo had already encircled him. He was soon struck down inside the fence of spears.

149

67
THE CASE OF KANSUKE NYUDO

BOTH ARMIES ENTERED full-scale battles around eight in the morning, and by noon a maelstrom raged on the plain. The shouts of mortal combat did not cease for an instant.

The Iron Wall of the Koshu army was said to have never experienced a collapse in any melee, but their formation and even Ushikubo's soldiers collapsed. Seeing each warrior fighting his own desperate struggle alone, every man in the Koshu army could not help resigning himself to the total defeat of the allied army with the thought, This is it.

Ushikubo-shu was a black unit that began with the birth of Mikawa Ushikubo and organized by all the brave generals and soldiers from the same district starting with Yamamoto Douki Nyudo, Osaragi Shozaemon, and Isahaya Goro. Their bamboo hats, helmets, full armor, and banners were all black from top to bottom.

"The time of our collapse will be the time of the total annihilation of the Koshu army" was the boast of the men of Ushikubo.

Was today that day at last?

The Ushikubo unit scrambled to escape. There were no witnesses, but the commander General Yamamoto Kansuke died in battle in the free-for-all.

According to an investigation conducted by the Echigo side after the war, it took four men to kill Yamamoto Nyudo. They were retainers of Kakizaki Izumi-no-kami: Hagita Yosobei, Yoshida Kishiro, Kouta Gunbei, and Sakanoki Isohachi.

The location was an area near Numagi Myojin shrine at Tofuku-ji Temple. His head was washed in a place called Mizusawa in Hachimanbara. The Buddhist priest there to wash the head did not wash only one head but the heads of three men. One of the heads was said to be the severed head of Yamamoto Nyudo because it resembled him. Thus, doubt lingered inside the Uesugi clan of "In the end, it is not clear whether it was the severed head of

Kansuke Nyudo."

Even the presence or absence of the man Yamamoto Kansuke had been a problem for a long time. In *Buko Zakki* (*Notes on Military Success*), a story was written about Kamiizumi Ise-no-kami and his disciple Kohaku returning home to Kyoto and meeting Yamamoto Kansuke at the Makino clan in Mikawa Ushikubo. In *Hokuetsu Gunki* (*Hokuetsu Military Notes*), he was written about like he was there and like he wasn't. As the arbitrator of Shingen's military law, he stipulated in *Koyo Gunkan*, the record of military exploits of the Takeda clan:

> Baba Mino shall be called the Creator of the Military Force. He
> shall assess the military camps of the other province. Consult with
> Hara Hayato about the battle formations.

In other words, the name of Yamamoto Kansuke could not be hidden as a military tactician inside the curtains of the field headquarters.

How much of what was written in *Koyo Gunkan* and *Buko Zakki* was true? In the end, only so much.

The only regret was having no way to record in minute detail the final moments of the man Kansuke.

68
A LINE OF BLOOD

PERHAPS, A SPARK from a gun ignited dry leaves, or a wildfire broke out from fire kicked around in the camp. Whatever the cause, smoke flowed like ink in the skies over a stretch of Kawanakajima.

Near two in the afternoon, smoke engulfed the sun like a grain of coral.

Beginning with the brave warrior Hajikano Gengoro, the deaths in battle of famous fighters were heard about one after the other. In addition to Shingen's younger brother Tenkyu Nobushige, the samurai generals Morozumi, Yamamoto, and Naito had been shot in succession. Also, the encampment of Koshu's force was seen immediately before its complete annihilation.

Kenshin struck his saddle and said, "My wish for many years will now be achieved." He looked back at the hatamoto surrounding him.

Of course, he had not yet decided on a fixed position for the camp since the morning.

He fomented waves of anger and galloped with no resistance in all directions.

In front and behind his horse, keeping a constant distance from the figure of the lord were, needless to say, the twelve hatamoto he selected at the start of the descent from Mount Kasuga.

He saw seven or eight faces including Chisaka Naizen, Ichikawa Shuzen, Okuni Heima, but later several of them had been injured or killed in battle and were soon no longer seen around Kenshin.

"Go. Don't fall behind," Kenshin called back over his shoulder.

He applied the whip to Hojo, his fine palomino horse. Takeda Taro Yoshinobu watched Kenshin gallop like a meteor toward him and into his troops.

"Where is your lord?"

"Just as I thought, you've made up your mind to achieve your impossible

152

wish."

The hatamoto kept galloping forward. Of course, Kenshin in front and the soldiers on foot did not reach the uninhabited field. They were blocked from the front, attacked from the sides, and hemmed in from behind. They formed a line of blood to swiftly advance by kicking wildly, pushing down, and stepping over.

In no time, another scattered unit suddenly rose up in a streak like a raging torrent behind Kenshin and his force of hatamoto.

This clash was surely reminiscent of the following passage from *Koyo Gunkan*.

> Enemies and allies, three thousand six or seven hundred men, will descend into mayhem and clash, shoot and be shot, and grapple with fully-armored shoulders and fall over. If a head is taken and raised, that head will be the lord's. Thrust out a spear to get it back, leap to kill. Even the sixteen- and seventeen-year-old pages and sandal bearers will form units and take action. Fight hand to hand to eventually stab and grab topknots. In the end, they won't be said to be hopeless as an enemy or an ally.

At last, Takeda Taro Yoshinobu's unit broke through. Stunned and basking in the scene of this disaster, Kenshin was galloping with a vengeance into the central force of Shingen he spotted that morning.

69

LIGHTNING IN A SUDDEN SHOWER

KENSHIN LEANED OVER as much as possible on the horse to lie prone but could not dodge the arrows and bullets. He thought, Shingen is close.

Until Kenshin saw him, he was determined not to alert his adversary or to cross swords with any enemy other than Shingen. Therefore, his disguise was more austere than his camp uniform. He wore a vest of yellowish-green silk damask tied with black armor braid. Only his face was exposed by the white silk *gyonin-zutsumi* hood wrapped around his head like a monk in battle. None of the magnificence of a general was perceptible.

However, his horse was the famous horse Hojo. His long sword *Azuki Nagamitsu* was nearly two and a half feet long.

"Where is Shingen?"

As his eyes searched like beacons, he galloped closer to the grounds of Hachiman.

When he came here, an unexpected enemy did not follow. Several officers and soldiers with bloodshot eyes brushed past, but not one saw him as the great enemy general Kenshin, and he took no notice of them.

He only asked himself whether he would face Shingen as he stepped over the banners, spears, and weapons lying on the fallen cedar leaves.

At that time, Takeda Shingen watched the enemy's move that crushed Taro Yoshinobu's troops and then passed like a whirlwind into Hachiman forest.

"What has the enemy planned next?"

Suspiciously, three master monk warriors and several hatamoto stood agitated in a group.

A strange shout bellowed nearby. When the faces turned in unison to the sound, "Shingen, are you there?" asked the figure of a large man who took huge strides like a savage beast and appeared to grow too large to be seen by two eyes.

154

Ah! That's Kenshin!

That was the intuition of the men present. Of the warriors inside the curtained field headquarters, although surely close to the lord, none held weapons like spears and pole arms with sword blades. The shocked adversaries didn't have the space to draw their swords.

"I'll get him," said one warrior monk and hurled a stool at Kenshin.

Did I hit him? Did I miss? The warrior couldn't tell where the stool went. Cedar leaves simply fell like rain. He wondered, Was Kenshin's figure on horseback supported by a drooping branch of the large cedar tree. When the palomino Hojo bent down to leap, his legs kicked into the crowd.

A single cry echoed, "Eeyah!"

Was that sound from Kenshin's mouth? Or was it the sound of Azuki Nagamitsu swinging down? In an instant, one warrior monk staggered backward cut the cords of the curtained enclosure with the tip of his sword and fell onto his back. He was not Shingen. He had gotten away but closely watched the figure of Kenshin, like a fierce tiger lurking in the bushes.

No, it could not be said his eyes saw him. Kenshin glimpsed to the right, turned his body left as he extended his long sword, and again shouted, "Eeyah!"

The next voice surely came from the pit of Kenshin's stomach. Shingen thrust out the iron military fan in his right hand and slightly sunk his front toward his left shoulder.

His numb hand tossed away the fan. When he changed his body's position like a mythical bird rising and clutched the hilt of his long sword, Kenshin's long sword sliced the air after he turned.

His move was clumsy.

Hara Osumi, the head of the lesser servants, picked up a spear with a blue shell shaft dropped there.

"Uh!" he released the grunt like he was biting down and came running. With his lord Shingen in danger, in a hair's breadth, he thrust his spear at the enemy on horseback.

Without looking away, Kenshin said, "You coward!"

On the third swing of his sword, his horse tried to leap over Shingen.

Shingen holding his injured right arm reversed his body and seemed to look back.

Over his back shoulder, his eyes caught the glare of the brightness of Azuki Nagamitsu. At almost the same moment, Hojo neighed and reared raising its legs high. In a rush, Hara Osumi's spear thrust missed.

"Dammit!"

He adjusted his grip on the broken spear and struck the triceps of Kenshin's horse with all his might.

70
HATAMOTO VERSUS HATAMOTO

"I CAN'T SEE him."

"Where is he?"

"Has he been killed in battle?"

Eight or nine hatamoto including Chisaka Naizen, Wada Hyoubu, Okuni Heima, and Demon Kojima Yataro were on foot and lost sight of Lord Kenshin.

"We never left his side, but the lord disappeared alone among the enemy. There's a chance we will be ridiculed for generations to come."

Nearly out of their minds, they ran around and resembled trees baying in a violent storm. They searched while shouting, "Lord! Lord!"

Out of nowhere, Imokawa Heidayu and Nagai Genshiro, two samurai from the same unit, came running like small birds blown from the sky in a typhoon and flew at full speed into the shadows of the curtained headquarters.

"Oh, Heidayu …"

"The lord was in that area, too."

Each man competed to enter the enclosure. In addition to the twelve Uesugi hatamoto, Takeda hatamoto running in confusion between nearby enemy huts and field headquarters were stopped in their tracks by the strange sound in the camp where Lord Shingen sat, and all converged on the same place.

As they closed in, Kenshin's hatamoto and Shingen's hatamoto swarmed together nearly knocking into each other. However, almost none of them realized the enemy was beside him.

Takeda's hatamoto focused on a chance encounter with Shingen. Uesugi's hatamoto worried about Kenshin's safety. Before the burning eyes and the terrifying postures on both sides, they thought about nothing other than the fates of their lords.

156

The lone rider Kenshin galloped into Shingen's camp and saw Shingen. In vain, he quickly swung Azuki Nagamitsu twice but only lightly wounded Shingen's right arm, slowed down his enemy Hara Osumi who hit the flank of his horse with the shaft of the spear. Kenshin managed to stay on his palomino Hojo who reared up then galloped sideways from the camp.

"Ah!"

What happened next could be said to be fortunate in the indescribable confusion. Perhaps, a tree root made the horse stumble and send him tumbling forward. Kenshin fell with force from the horse.

Hara Osumi and others chased with several spears.

"Good!"

They scrambled to see Kenshin's figure and leaped at him.

"Ah! He's in danger."

Uesugi's hatamoto seemed to ignore something and took off running to his side.

"Go!"

They lined up their spearheads to block the way.

Meanwhile, Hojo ran with an empty saddle wildly into the camp of Nagasaki Chokan.

Demon Kojima Yataro grabbed the muzzle of a random horse and went to Kenshin. In no time, he leaped onto the horse and snapped the whip.

As Kenshin called to his hatamoto, "Go back. Go back!" he managed to cleave the enemy throng again and run back to his allies.

71
ECHOING VOICES

HE LEFT QUICKLY as quickly as he came.

Why did Kenshin hastily withdraw? His hatamoto and the enemy's hatamoto made a fence of spears and fell into frenzied mortal combat. Hara Osumi on Takeda's side shouted many times, "This time will be remembered as the allies' chance for victory. And the detached force coming from Mount Saijo last night, and the units of Kousaka, Baba, Amari, and Oyamada will hurtle in like a swift cloud!"

Kenshin made a snap judgment this morning on whether there would be victory or defeat and never stopped worrying in his heart about the movements of the ten detached forces of Takeda.

He made a regrettable swing of his long sword at the enemy general Shingen. Kenshin's central army could be said to have been trampled. A part of his long-held hope pent up for many years was released. He considered *this place* to be the *turning point* in the military maneuver and abruptly made a clean retreat.

When Kenshin withdrew, Ichikawa Shuzen, Chisaka Naizen, Wada Hyoubu, and Imokawa Heidayu also made a run for the allies following his trail.

As they ran out, only the loudest voices of Imokawa Heidayu and Demon Kojima Yataro carried.

"Imokawa Heidayu will kill and take the head of Takeda Daizen Daifu Harunobu."

"The Uesugi samurai Demon Kojima Yataro and Imokawa Heidayu will combine strength to kill and take the head of Shingen. Measly warriors of Takeda don't block the road where his head will pass."

Of course, this was a lie.

However, Hara Osumi showed nothing more than his quick wit when he shouted, "The allied detached force on Mount Saijo is not far away."

At that time, this exchange of words exhibited a combat force surpassing the actions of bodies.

When opposing forces mixed together in fights with spears, on horseback, and with swords, chaotically bathed in blood, and gripping each other's flesh, a fight surely was not a silent affair. Rather, enemies and allies shouted stinging curses and shrieks back and forth. But most of the shouts had no meaning. One warrior had the habit of fighting while chanting Buddhist prayers. Voices chanting, "I pray the power of the Goddess of Mercy shatters the sword of my true enemy and protects my life," could be heard in the fray. Young warriors repeatedly chanted the names of ancestors inscribed in their hearts like magic spells. That wasn't all, daredevil warriors attacked while belching out the grunts heard when chopping wood or when starting to row a large boat with oars.

Sounds poured from all mouths whether conscious or not. As they merged, if the samurai could say the right words to move the enemies' spirits and rouse the morale of the allies at the perfect moment, he could be said to be an exceptional veteran of many battles or the right man possessing both courage and wit.

On this day, violent winds had been blowing since noon. The figures of men and horses on both sides became nearly invisible in dense clouds of sand and dust. One might have believed it was night, despite the sun in the sky. Later, when this time was recalled, the awful clouds of dust were remembered.

The hooves of the military horses repeatedly dug up the earth only to be kicked up again by the soldiers.

Adding to the confusion, wild rumors flew back and forth. In times like this, many soldiers in both the Takeda and the Uesugi forces killed their comrades.

One particular rumor of "Lord Shingen has been killed" spread among Takeda's army like a talisman. In no time, shades of dismay and desolation blanketed the entire force.

Finally, that rumor became known in Shingen's headquarters where his camp stool was restored to his customary place for comfort. Naito Shuri passed on official notices only on serious matters while riding his horse to allied positions.

"The lord is fine. What order is safe? If an ally is caught up in lies about the enemy and their morale is disturbed, kill and throw them away."

Trembling of the entire army from anxiety was finally quieted by this notice, but the central unit of Takeda once right in the middle of the central army trampled under the hooves of Kenshin's horse was unable to speedily recover from the surprise and the disruption of their battle formation.

However, great patience was endured only for Takeda Shingen. Soon there was good news about the Koshu army who fought a hard defensive battle.

"I can see them. A force of ten units is coming from over there, and from downstream and upstream on the Chikuma," shouted a lookout high up a tree in Hachiman forest. The commanders below relayed this report via shouts to Shingen's camp.

72

A CHANGE IN THE STATE OF WAR

THEY WERE TOO late.

The support from allied forces that shifted from Mount Saijo was too late.

Starting with Shingen, all officers and soldiers engaged in the hard fight wondered, What's happening?

At this point, they were filled with rage.

When they headed to Mount Saijo and saw Kenshin was gone, they knew they were facing an inane, hopeless enemy.

The thick fog from morning until noon was one reason they had no clue about the heading of Uesugi's force. They cautiously moved to their next action because Uesugi's tactic might be a ruse.

Also, when they descended the mountain and crossed the river, Amakasu Oumi-no-kami known by all as a brave general of Uesugi commanded the zone of Junikase from a small hill in the small forest on the opposite shore. But they were prepared with a tactic from Sun Tzu's *The Art of War*.

If the enemy crosses a river, hit them in the center of the river.

A long time passed before the counselors heard distant gunshots coming from Kawanakajima. The hope was to be shrouded by dense fog and dust kicked up by horses as the battle cries rose.

"Dammit. The enemy's main force has been attacked by an undermanned main force of the allies. We can't delay."

Two groups began to wade across upstream and downstream. Unlike a horseman crossing alone, preparations and time are needed.

The number of soldiers here in the detached unit far outnumbered Shingen's main force that left Hachimanbara earlier. A total force of twelve thousand men was split into ten units under ten commanders.

In that case, Kenshin warned that this cluster of clouds moving from Mount Saijo was the most reasonable action. As a defense, Amakasu Oumi-no-kami occupied the hill in the small forest since the morning.

"Now!" was all he said.

Before the enemy stepped foot on this shore, arrows and bullets rained down on them.

The water surface within the range of the bullets splashed like hit by raindrops during showers. The water turned a deep red as an unknown number of fallen soldiers bobbed up and down in the current.

At first, Kenshin looked like he would make most of the gun units in the force stay behind here. From the beginning, his unit prepared for the amputation strategy because they expected arrows and bullets to be useless.

However, they were not inexperienced troops who would flinch but were prepared to sacrifice themselves from the beginning. The units under Baba Minbu and Amari Saemon came galloping up from downstream. The units of Oyamada Bitchu, Obata Yamashiro, and Sanada Danjo came ashore upstream.

This time, the actions of Amakasu Oumi-no-kami from Echigo and his men were remarkable. Everyone is well aware that Amakasu would enter the Uesugi clan in the distant future. Regrettably, even hard fighting by a portion of the troops in a unit unconnected to this army would never be able to hold off a surge of twelve thousand warriors for long.

The enemy force projected from upstream reached Hachimanbara in no time. They merged with Yamamoto Douki's unit pushed back to the edge of death. The enemy force facing them and flush with their victory over the Kakizaki clan of Echigo swiftly counterattacked, pursued, and routed them.

The fresh troops of the Koshu force who came from downstream steadily pushed forward to pressure the back of Uesugi's force. In response to the battle cries of the main army near Hachiman Shrine, the location of Shingen, war cries with a new strength rose from a corner of the plain in a ferocious attack on the flank of Uesugi's force.

The Naoe, Yasuda, and Aragawa clans charged on horseback to this place.

Angry waves pushed and were pushed back. Blood spurted all around in endless sprays.

73
THE SUN DARKENS

"YATARO, YATARO."

"Yes."

"Plant the banner here."

"Yessir."

Kenshin abandoned his horse and stood on the plain. They were far behind allied lines.

When Demon Kojima Yataro raised the Bishamon and the Hinomaru banners high, Kenshin gave the order, "Sound the shell," to Uno Samanosuke, the conch-shell trumpeter.

He didn't say what conch signal to blow, but the trumpeter Samanosuke knew. And now five or six of the lord's hatamoto like Okuni Heima, Wada Kihei, and Ichikawa Shuzen ran out in all directions to relay the lord's order "Pull back now."

"War has come this far!"

As the wind blew over his uncooled face moist with sweat, Kenshin grumbled loudly, "Kakizaki Izumi and other allies who penetrated deep into the area near Hirose are agitated. Is notification by only conch shells adequate?"

Chisaka Naizen's face tensed from worry as he stretched himself tall.

Perhaps ..., Kenshin might have thought, too, because the allies there crossed the Chikuma and their retreat was blocked by the main force of the Koshu army and the fresh troops of the enemy force.

"No, it will be all right. Izumi-no-kami will surely punch sideways through the new enemy troops to reach them. In that case, Amakasu is in the small forest. The units of Naoe Yamato-no-kami, Yasuda, and Aragawa will coalesce into one and withdraw."

In the end, the events unfolded as he said. The allies gradually made their way back to camp.

163

The reversal could not be hidden. Kenshin obviously believed his forces would win. Now with the addition of twelve thousand fresh troops for Shingen, Kenshin's only choice was for the allies to put down their weapons. He changed to submission, a complete reversal from the morning.

Did he realize he had pushed his luck by attacking to his heart's content and would probably be hotly pursued the next time?

No, if it goes wrong, this moment may see the annihilation of the allies. Once the battle position altered the landscape of victory and defeat, Shingen's face displayed that much savagery. However, Kenshin's face was serene. As he looked all around at his banners and the allies withdrawing, this thought was in his heart.

"I won. I have no doubt I won.... But can I say this win was a win I somehow managed to secure or an absolute win?"

He had seen war, but the battle with Takeda's army finally began for him. When he shielded his eyes, like during a solar eclipse, to look up at the sky, it was around four in the afternoon.

74
THE UNKNOWN KENSHIN

OTHERS WERE THERE. Nearly ten warriors were on horseback.

They faced the red sun in the west.

Dusk began to slide over the grassy plain grazed by a dismal moaning wind. The unit of nearly ten unknown warriors on horseback raised their banners and looked all around. They could see a single, large character representing the Buddhist deity Bishamon (毘) on a white background.

"The enemy."

"A good general," Kenshin said as the Takeda force galloped toward them not knowing who he was.

The warriors in that group were swiftly closing in on Kenshin, but the Takeda men probably didn't notice him.

"Is that Shibata? One of Kakizaki's men?"

It appeared a few allies recognized the banner and promptly came. When they were about one hundred steps away, Nagai Genjiro beside Kenshin said, "It's Kousaka." At first, the group was taken by surprise and reflexively moved to protect the lord.

Kousaka Masanobu's followers numbered two or three hundred warriors about ten times the number of Kenshin's hatamoto. Luckily, however, the group in Kousaka's force was not the main force.

"His head" was Kenshin's objective and he began his attack but was not a leader with a belief in precise aim. By chance, he spotted a small clump of enemy soldiers and only hoped to annihilate them.

"They're ordinary soldiers."

The men protecting Kenshin fought their best.

Nagai Genjiro, Takemata Choshichi, and Demon Kojima Yataro were roused then plunged into the enemy. This small force confronted being engulfed by the larger number of rival soldiers, ducked, and protected and defended the narrow stretch of land. Their self-reliance alone defeated being

165

captured by the enemy.

The enemy was no match for this throng and soon scattered before the driving advance led by Nagai, Demon Kojima, and Takemata.

A few figures savagely holding spears and wearing long swords seemed to pursue them, but only superior hatamoto from the Echigo force surrounded Kenshin.

It was nothing special. While swinging their long swords and blades attached to long poles to scatter the men they targeted, they exchanged a torrent of shouts and howls.

The small number of ten allies scattered, which put them at a disadvantage. Their positions to shield Lord Kenshin crumbled. Also, Kenshin was on horseback.

Uno Samanosuke and Chisaka Naizen grabbed the muzzle of Kenshin's horse and ran. Inaba Hikoroku, Wada Hyoubu, Iwai Toshiro, and the others ran after them killing any enemy who came too close then stopped to regroup and form the rear guard.

75

THE GENERAL OF A WOUNDED ARMY IS LIKE A MOTHER'S HEART

KENSHIN'S HORSE DIDN'T stop until he reached the banks of the Sai River.

A little before one in the morning, only his horse's hooves kicked at the Koshu headquarters. He had given a flash of light onto Shingen's head but did not grind his teeth in hesitation when he withdrew. He looked unmoved.

"Wait, Chisaka, wait."

Naizen stopped pulling his horse into the rapids to cross the river. Once again, Kenshin stopped his horse beside him.

"Is he there?"

Okuni Heiba and Ichigawa Shuzen returned to his side after going out earlier to the allies at various locations to pass on the general order to withdraw.

As he lingered, he prevented Kousaka's unit from taking the lead. Finally, Demon Kojima, Nagai, Takemata, and several others found a way out and gathered here all stained red.

Ten then twenty other Echigo allies slowly joined them. However, they held a variety of positions in various branches of the military. Despite seeing that, Kenshin wondered whether the main force of the allies and each unit were being torn apart and fighting desperately at each location and falling into confusion on all fronts.

Water babbled and dismal winds blew as dusk moved in with a piercing cold air. Painful grief invaded Kenshin's heart for the officers and men under his command who would never return.

"What happened to Shibata Naganori, Shinzu Tango. Honjo Echizen-no-kami, and Hojo Akino? Kakizaki probably found a withdrawal route. Naoe is …"

That man who appeared to be a god of war who would destroy a demon looked around the plain at nightfall and grumbled, his intensity was like a mother who came out through the gate to wait for a child late in returning home.

"He's all right. Don't worry," said Okuni Heiba to encourage him.

"The back-up enemy troops from Mount Saijo of powerful soldiers and fresh troops provided general support. Gradually, all the allies withdrew in the direction of the Sai River and Tamba Island. You know that some units may be unaware they are already standing in the area of the lord, crossed the Sai River, and retreated far to the rear."

Following Heiba's words, everyone complained to Kenshin.

"The number who came here may be countless. Instead, they may have become confused by the gathering of the allies."

"They probably crossed the Sai River a little earlier and retreated to safe territory."

"They wouldn't come back to this dangerous place."

Kenshin allowed this rebuke. In that case, they should cross the river and redirect their horses to the dry riverbed.

His horses' legs stood on a shoal called Tamba Island and men waded in upstream sinking nearly to their necks. The waters downstream filled an abyss.

The Chikuma River flowed gently, and its rapids were shallow. In contrast, the Sai River was a rushing torrent. At the height of summer in July, the amount of water in this stretch of the river was at its shallowest. September and October was the rainy season in the mountains. The actual situation in a typical year was a rapid increase in the water level of about four to five feet. Shallows allowing men to wade across existed nowhere, especially downstream of Tamba Island.

Kenshin worried about his fears and repeatedly muttered, "A withdrawal route."

Most of all, several allied commanders knew the depths along this stretch of the river. At the same time, Takeda's generals shared that common knowledge.

Consequently, while the enemy stood on a dominant position, they were believed to be directing the brunt of their attack and their siege downstream on the Sai River.

Kenshin and his hatamoto commanded more than one hundred men. Earlier, around ten warriors left Kenshin behind to enter and slosh through the river using their spears as canes. They searched the shallows to find a path to escort their lord.

However, their guide through the water suddenly splashed in the river and toppled over.

It wasn't a gunshot. They thought they heard the snap of a bowstring echo nearby.

An elite soldier of the Koshu force commanded by Takeda Taro

Yoshinobu shouted, "Forward."

"Take the lead."

The raid swept in like a gale. Kousaka's troops were being assaulted from the front and withstood an incomparably bloody squall. They were charged with anger close to madness.

Some entered the water up to their shins; Kenshin was on the dry riverbed. A mist formed naturally, and the men in the river returned.

Takemata Choshichi cut down the first fierce enemy, grappled with the enemy following close behind, somersaulted over, and rolled to the water's edge.

"Dammit!"

He stood up among the blood and immediately ran into a mob of Koshu soldiers. The armor tassets were gone from one sleeve. His helmet was lost, and his hair lifted up in the wind.

Honda Ukonjo fought a strong Koshu general as Kenshin watched. It was a clash between eagles.

The pair of Wada Hyoubu and Uno Samanosuke always met one enemy after another with two spears.

One thrust of the spear. Was this another minor fighting strategy?

Every last page near Kenshin was smeared with fresh blood.

Of the one hundred or more men, forty to fifty men were killed in a heartbeat.

A pile of enemy corpses stacked up.

Moreover, retreating and backing away were not easy.

The father Shingen was wounded. At one time, Taro Yoshinobu on the verge of the annihilation of his force gained fresh troops and recouped.

"If this shame of the early war can't be washed away, I am too humiliated to live and face the people of Koshu" reflected the heroic spirit held by the leader and his elite troops. At this time the water surface was already dark in the twilight. Regrettably, in time Taro Yoshinobu eluded Kenshin who stood before his eyes unaware the man was Uesugi Kenshin.

76

IN DYING THERE IS LIFE

KENSHIN APPLIED THE whip again to the horse's belly and ran off.

Was this evening's fog blood? A dread drifted in like blowing ink on the surface of the harvest moon.

"Is Samanosuke here?"

"I think he's at the Mimaki field shallows."

"He probably retreated further back."

Discouraged, he looked at the moon from his horse. Kenshin repeatedly blinked one eye. The blood pouring from his forehead to his cheek started drying in his eyelashes and blocked his vision.

"You got him? The one following me."

"I think so."

Samanosuke was also gloomy, but Kenshin's shoulders began to shake as if amused.

"If we can cross the river, we will go to the foot of Mount Takanashi and leave this strip of Nakano plain. In that case, we'll cross. Samanosuke, watch the rapids."

"Yessir."

That area didn't appear particularly deep. Samanosuke tugged on the muzzle to gently lead the horse to the river.

The water was as cold as ice.

White waves washed the saddle.

Kenshin muttered like he was reciting a prayer.

"In dying there is life. In living there is no life. Aah, it's a treasure, so important. Remember the chill of the water in autumn. I don't think I'll die."

> In dying there is life.
> In living there is no life.

He often repeated these words in any situation and told this story to his vassals.

Kenshin was twenty-four or -five years old when he met an elderly priest in the castle town of Mount Kasuga.

"Priest, where are you going?" asked Kenshin from his horse. The priest was Souken of Rinsenji Temple. He lifted his head high to look up and replied, "Where is the castle lord?"

"Maybe, he left for the battlefield," said Kenshin.

"I'm not sure," the priest only quickly bowed his head and left to join some people by the side of the road.

Kenshin jumped off his horse and called to Honjo Seishichiro, a samurai attendant.

"Go after the priest I just spoke to. Apologize for my crime of arrogance. In a word, tell him to pray for my sake."

Apologize? thought an annoyed Seishichiro, who was about to go to war, but followed Souken and told him.

Souken felt deeply obliged and returned, but thought, I have no teachings. If I answer as a country priest, what will be the answer? He lingered for a short time with the sleeves of his arms crossed.

Still dismounted, Kenshin politely asked for a prayer.

"Can you say something like advance the warriors with Godspeed? Like a rule to spread sacred teachings?"

"In the advance of warriors, death goes first. In the spread of the teachings, death goes first. Today, all know only life and not death. It doesn't matter. The past and the future only cross paths."

"I have one more question."

"Yes."

"Look at the weak and retreat and move toward the strong. Is it the other way? Is that the order?"

"A man who does not fear death is at ease, and one who enjoys life is dangerous. Everyone is found among the strong or the weak, advancing or retreating, and in the enlightenment of life and death. What about you, Lord?" the priest asked the question for a change looking for an answer.

Kenshin was silent for a short time but finally answered, "In dying there is life. In living there is no life."

Hearing this, the priest Souken laughed loudly.

"Very well.... Goodbye."

Kenshin bowed and left the camp.

He returned later in triumph and entered Rinsenji Temple incognito to visit the kind Priest Souken and to gain further insight. Kenshin is said to have named himself using the same kanji character for *ken* meaning humility found in the name Souken. A look at the diary of him as a young man kept by his private secretary revealed that he always went alone into the stateroom in the inner citadel. Everyone else waited in the distinguished visitor's room to avoid interrupting his Zen studies.

One could guess he was absorbed in Zen, and his spiritual guide was Souken, the seventh generation at Rinsenji Temple.

His devotion was not confined to Zen; each of Shintoism, Confucianism, and Buddhism reached deep into his heart. He discerned the foolish man among men who fear Heaven and Earth. Even in Buddhism, he studied without discrimination the teachings of the Jodo sect, the Hokke sect, the Tendai sect, and the Shin sect and drew out their essence to fill his spiritual vessel.

77

A PERFECT PULSE

FROM HACHIMANBARA TO the vast plain of Tamba Island, the evening moon came out, but the battle cries did not stop.

Only sparks flew all around from the long swords and spears clashing at their ridges like countless fish jumping between waves of the forces screaming at each other. Despite the colors of the warriors' uniforms and hoods and the shadows of the banners, it was unclear who was an enemy and who was an ally.

The fresh supply of Takeda's troops from the units of Kousaka, Amari, Oyamada, Yamamoto, Baba, and Sanada encircled various places to annihilate Uesugi's force in the center. Nevertheless, the confusion of Uesugi's force put a great deal of pressure on the new and powerful Koshu force that rotated in from Mount Saijo.

Inside were fifteen hundred of Uesugi's troops in perfect order. Troops under the command of Amakasu Oumi-no-kami were moving in a gradual withdrawal from the vicinity of the small forest. As Retreat! Retreat! rang from the conch shells, the scattered allied gathered together, the enemy striking the flanks was hit and pulled back with dignity to Sai River.

"That is a splendid withdrawal," remarked the enemies Sanada and Kousaka seeing them off. What were their two units thinking as they swiftly retraced their path back to Kaizu Castle?

Later, inside the Koshu army, the pullback of the two units of Sanada and Kousaka was an evacuation for some reason. Shingen decided, "Seeing the victory of seventy percent of the allies, the retreat during safety was brilliant and not to be criticized."

By this time, Shingen's main force cleared out of the temple at Hachiman, crossed at Hirose pass that morning, and left Kawanakajima with every last hatamoto. Therefore, there was no reason to leave the battlefield before the main force.

173

Later, the mass of men remaining was that day's wounded and the war dead. The only human figures working in the area covered in evening dew were the soldiers who remained behind after carrying the corpses and the wounded to their respective army.

On the shore of the Sai River, Amakasu Oumi-no-kami set up a huge banner and waited for the allies to gather as the bellowing of the conch shell continued for a short time.

The remnants of the defeated army who had been yearning for that sound numbered more than three thousand and streamed in from every direction. They eventually crossed the river to the north and camped at Kuzuno.

As a result of the bloody battle that began in the morning and lasted more than seven or eight hours, the deaths in battle of the two armies were recorded as:

Koshu deaths in battle - 4,630
Echigo deaths in battle - 3,470

Despite these numbers, in the Koshu army, both Takeda Shingen and his son Taro Yoshinobu were wounded. The indisputable fact was many of the top generals of the clan, Tenkyu Nobushige, Morozumi Bungo-no-kami, Yamamoto Douki, and Ogasawara Wakasa, died or were wounded in battle, while not one Uesugi general was killed. The wounded and dead of Uesugi came from the time fresh troops were added by the enemy's rotation force on Mount Saijo. Almost all of the Takeda dead and wounded were from the lower ranks used to lure and trap the enemy inside the tumultuous rout. Another cause was the foolhardy rush into the deep currents of the Sai River downstream of Tamba Island where they drowned and were pierced by arrows.

78
A LONELY FIGURE

IN THE SHADOW of the moon were the master and his follower.

Only the sounds of insects could be heard. No homes or flickering lights were found in this area, only thick fog and grass that hid the great battle that day.

"There aren't any houses around here, are there?"

"We may find one along the way."

"Samanosuke, you're probably cold."

"Because I walk leading the horse by his muzzle, naturally, I forget about the cold.... Although you're riding, Lord, you got drenched and are chilled, too."

"I want a fire.... I will remember the unforgettable cold of this autumn."

In the Mimaki field, the master and his follower crossed the river to search for a field of fire while leaving behind tears on the road they walked.

Kenshin suddenly stopped his horse.

"Is that an ally? Someone seems to be calling from behind," he said and turned.

Holding onto the horse's muzzle, Samanosuke strained to see. Under the white moon, a man was running, almost dancing, toward them. They could hear his heavy breathing as he neared.

"Lord, is the lord here?"

"Ah, Wada Kihei?"

"Yes, yes."

The moment he saw the lord was safe, Kihei dropped down onto his buttocks. He also crossed to this side by plunging into the river and was a wet mouse, but the blood was not washed from his head and face.

"What happened to the others?" Kenshin asked.

Kihei gathered himself to answer, "Wada Hyoubu stood his ground and was stab by the great force of the enemy and met his end."

175

"Was Hyoubu killed in battle, too?"

"And Uno Yogoro ..." he started to say but equivocated as he saw Samanosuke's face beside the horse's muzzle. Uno Yogoro was Samanosuke's younger brother.

"Wada, is Yogoro gone?"

The older brother's complexion gave the unavoidable answer.

"His actions inside the melee were astounding. I painfully witnessed him suffering serious wounds at several places on his body. I carried him on my shoulder here to the rapids at Mimaki. When we reached the center of the river he said, '... In the end, despite following the lord, my body hinders my service to him. My time has come. I will say goodbye ...'"

"And then ..."

"In an instant, he tore away from my grip, left my shoulder and drowned himself in the raging current. I shouted and screamed but he was silent and gone."

Samanosuke tilted his face up and answered to the moon, "... I see."

Kenshin silently urged his horse with the reins. On that night, the lonely figure of a commander who had been surrounded by thirteen thousand troops left the battlefield with two vassals. What were the strong emotions of the leader and his followers? The battlefield can be called a large training ground where Heaven and Earth become the temple. Although slight, the color of defeat was not visible on Kenshin's face whitened by the moon. Rather one could infer from his relaxed lips his total ease after completing the task and an eagerness for serious ideas for the next battle.

79

WOLVES

"**AH! I SEE** a light."

At long last, Samanosuke, who was on foot, caught sight of a home and reported to Kenshin on the horse.

"No, it's not firelight from a farmhouse," said Kenshin shaking his head.

When he said that, flames blazed a little too much to be simple lamplight or fire for cooking at a farmhouse.

"Of course, it's as you say, someone has built a huge bonfire."

After moving forward another seven hundred to one thousand feet, Uno Samanosuke hesitated. Kenshin asked Wada Kihei to go scout the area.

"They wouldn't get this far. There's no reason for Takeda's force to scatter and come to this area. I think they're no different from groups of soldiers of fortune who prepared mentally for today's battle, stretched a net over the routes taken by fugitives, and are waiting for money."

"If they're soldiers of fortune, there are at most twenty to thirty. They are a rabble with a trifling number of rogues. Kihei and I will sweep the road clean. Lord, please relax and wait in the shadows of the trees."

When Samanosuke was about to gallop away, Kenshin said, "Stop. Stop," and turned his horse around to say, "We'll go further out and take a detour. Kihei, look for a narrow path.

The daring Kenshin kicked down the Iron Wall of several thousand troops of the Koshu force and galloped alone into a band of their hatamoto. But when he caught sight of the bonfire of soldiers of fortune blocking the road, he turned his horse to search for a safe byway.

That night, they crossed the Hoshina mountain path and took a short nap in the shadow of a big tree.

The next day, they crossed a rice field in the mountains nearly two and a half miles from Takaino and descended to the Sarashina region, centered around Obasuteyama, the mountain where legend says the elderly were abandoned.

Also on that evening, they encountered more soldiers of fortune, but with no escape route, Kihei and Samanosuke drove off the soldiers, and they passed through.

However, this pack of soldiers valued Kenshin's riding outfit and would tenaciously pursue him to the end of the world.

At twilight, Kenshin, Kihei, and Samanosuke came to a stretch of the river called the Yasuda Crossing. When they looked back, a short four hundred feet behind them the gang of soldiers of fortune raised a racket with their shouts and howls. Laughably, they came no closer and resembled a pack of wolves ready to pounce and bite in an unguarded moment.

"This will work. We'll pull the horses across."

A thick rope stretched from their bank to the other side of the river. The men and the horses rode on a raft tied below the rope.

Four or five figures appeared above on the bank behind them as they pulled the thick rope hand over hand to bring the raft to the center of the river. The soldiers were quick to follow.

"What are you barking about?"

The laughter from Kihei and Samanosuke on the raft spurred the flight of a couple of weary arrows. They also seemed to have guns but no bullets. The pair only saw many faces baring white teeth.

The raft leisurely arrived on the opposite shore.

As he mounted his horse, Kenshin gave the order, "Samanosuke, cut the crossing rope."

Samanosuke pulled out his long sword and sliced the rope. The thick rope drew a large arc, hit the water with a splash, and flowed in one direction.

The shadows of large hands of the ones with white teeth and the ones with heads shaped like pot cleaners again howled and cursed from the other embankment, and stomped the ground. This place was no longer a battlefield. It was the world.

80

BUCKWHEAT FLOWERS

As Kenshin traveled down Echigo Road, he wondered, Was this Yasuda Crossing? Was it somewhere else? Around twilight when they reached a road, he said, "The river appears to follow two paths over there. The course of the Chikuma River does not split in two. Did we go the wrong way?"

Wada Kihei laughingly answered, "Lord, you are exhausted. That is not the river. That is a field of buckwheat flowers blowing in the wind."

This story remained a topic of conversation in this region for many years to come.

After the tenth day of September according to the lunar calendar, buckwheat flowers were already late in blooming. The telling of this legend began right after the three men returned after the war to Mount Kasuga prompted by the sudden death of Wada Kihei.

What had they eaten on their journey home? As they traced their way to Kasugayama Castle, Kihei experienced terrible vomiting and diarrhea and died.

Kenshin remarked, "How wretched." Despite having administered medicine to him with his own hands, Kihei died.

The shame of his lifetime said to be a great general like Kenshin mistaking buckwheat flowers for a river might have been the reason for telling the story of Wada Kihei's spitting up blood and dying. The world's laughter could be heard all around. The rumor was Kenshin killed Kihei soon after they returned to the castle. There was no doubt.

This fabrication probably came from the Takeda side. Whether it did or not, this slander was absurd.

However, the path Kenshin and his followers took from Kawanakajima into Echigo certainly could be imagined to have presented unimaginable hardships. Sleep and food were hard to come by. Several legends along these lines are told in his native province, but most echo the tale of the buckwheat flowers.

81

TRACKS OF A STANDING BIRD

BEFORE THE SUSOHANA River southeast of Zenkoji Temple, Naoe Yamato-no-kami collected large and small packhorses. Warriors scattered from other units also gathered.

The day after the great battle as well as the next day, they stood their ground.

Amakasu Oumi-no-kami retreated to the Sai River and approached defeated remnant soldiers to establish direct contact. He dispatched warriors who flowed in from the broad plain of Kawanakajima to every corner of the nearby forest to bring every last dead and wounded allied warrior as well as the fragments of banners to the camp.

From the words of Chisaka Naizen, Imokawa Heidayu, and other hatamoto, it was assumed the lord returned home safely. They sometimes quarreled, without realizing it, over following Kenshin.

"Instead, you'll become the one to show the lord's route to the enemy," said Naoe Oumi-no-kami with enough force to stop them.

Kenshin was a serene man. Not only was this withdrawal maneuver important, but he also said it was preparation for the next army.

This day was the day after the war ended.

In the Koshu army far away from this predicament, beginning with Obata Yamashiro-no-kami, all the generals eager to fight came before Shingen to offer similar counsel and hope.

"Naoe and Amakasu are positioned at the nearby Susohana River, and soldiers of Uesugi's defeated army are gathering there. If we command our warriors to move and attack like a swift wind, they probably won't live to return to Echigo."

Shingen withheld his permission, he said, "Absolutely not, stopping was good. Despite suffering that serious wound, over three days, our self-possessed enemy stood on the stage of the battle before our camp. If we carelessly meddle and are bitten by a cornered mouse, I would become the laughingstock not them."

From the third to the fourth day, the Echigo force gradually pulled back with dignity and colors flying to the north in no way different from the time they arrived at this plain.

82

SHOUTS OF VICTORY

AFTER UESUGI'S FORCE cleared out, Hajikano Den'emon flew there and back by horse to investigate. He reported, "There wasn't even scattered evidence like a food container that's tied to a soldiers waist."

Shingen listened and said to all present, "If an enemy so cautious strikes, at least, it is certain the same number of allies was wounded."

However, several generals explained, "Until this end, after stepping onto the stage of this battlefield in Hachimanbara, the victory of the allies in this war was never in doubt. Holding a victory ceremony in the future is appropriate."

Shingen did not disagree with this opinion. It had been a disaster with the loss of his younger brother, several famous generals, and several thousand followers. He was wounded, and even his son Taro Yoshinobu suffered assorted wounds. However, he boasted of victory as a plausible truth and with a full heart.

"He was confused, and I was finished. He left, and I remained."

"The stage will be cleansed."

Shingen ordered them to prepare.

Kousaka Danjo and the other generals departed and met again at Kaizu.

The ritual required a wide expanse of land. The entire army formed ranks, stood in solemn lines, worshipped the god of war in the central pure land of shrines and temples, sprinkled saltwater, erected arrangements of sacred *sakaki* plants, and lit votive lights.

The assembly of generals in the curtained field headquarters was arranged by his role as follows and stood solemnly facing the altar.

Standard-bearer of the ancestors: Kousaka Danjo
Standard-bearer of the descendants: Yamagata Saburobei
Sacred arrow on the right: Oyamada Bitchu-no-kami

Sacred arrow on the left: Baba Minbu Shouyu
Military taiko drum: Atobe Oinosuke
Military conch shell: Nagasaka Chokan
Esteemed sword: Obu Hyobusho
Spear with pearl inlay: Obata Yamashiro-no-kami
Wooden clappers: Amari Saemon

At a position somewhat removed, the commander-in-chief Shingen sat on a camp stool with his clan and hatamoto behind him.

The split white cloth bandaging his right hand stood out. What was he teaching about the silent courage of the Koshu warrior?

Before the camp stool, a lone general respectfully handed a lacquered tray carrying celebratory side dishes. Shingen's left hand reached out to take one dried chestnut and snapped open his large signaling fan decorated with the sun and the moon.

Then he stood, looked at the sky and yelled out in triumph, "Aay! Aay! Oooooh!"

In response, the generals, their men, and the rank and file shouted, "Aay! Aay! Oooooh!"

They repeated these shouts of Glory! Honor! Yes! three times.

Peace in the world. Tranquility throughout the country. Safety of the people. Mortal enemies driven away.

The two sacred arrows sliced through the wind.

Again Heaven and Earth boomed with the shouts "Aay! Oooooh!" This time they were simple cheers and shouts of joy. The enthusiasm and the emotion in their bodies were released into the air. They were oblivious to the tears flowing down their cheeks. For unknown reasons, tears simply wetted both cheeks.

83

A FAIR AND JUST REPUTATION

AFTER THE FULL retreat to Mount Kasuga, Kenshin, all his men, and the entire Uesugi clan were certain of decisive victory by its force.

"The allies won."

"The enemies Shingen and his son were wounded."

"Great generals of the clan of Koshu fell side by side in battle. However, the enemy did not take the head of one allied general."

Similarly, the Takeda force chanted, "A great victory for the Koshu force!" over and over. They took a stand in Hachimanbara, went with pride to the victory ceremony, and then left for Kofu.

Was the great battle at Kawanakajima in Eiroku year 4 a clear victory for either Koshu or Echigo? Of course in the military caste, this became a subject of popular debate. Some said Kenshin won. Others said Shingen was the victor. At that time, boisterous but fair and just exchanges were already underway.

Ota Sukemasa Nyudo was one of at least five to seven military strategists who were famous generals in the warring states. The following assessment described their military strategies.

"At the onset of fighting at Kawanakajima during the morning starting at dawn, it is no exaggeration to say that Kenshin will be the victor with a certainty of eighty percent. By examining the battle formation, the vanguard of Uesugi's force will destroy up to the third or fourth line deep in Takeda's force. Based on his experience, Shingen boasted of there not being one example of the feet of the hatamoto in those ranks being stomped on by the enemy. Therefore, if he saw the lone horseman of Kenshin break through, he would have difficulty imagining that the Takeda army had momentarily fallen to a dangerous state of utter confusion.

"Not a few of his powerful generals fell side by side in battle. Shingen and his son were wounded, and even his younger brother Tenkyu Nobushige was killed in battle. There was no way to hide the fact that Takeda's side was driven one step closer to what could only be called disastrous ruin.... However, in the later battle that lasted from noon until evening, the situation reversed so much that the odds favored Shingen winning with the odds of ten to seven.

"This turning point was the change beginning the moment fresh troops arriving from Mount Saijo clashed from the side and left Uesugi's force gasping. The inevitability of Uesugi's total defeat was an intense surprise attack that divided the commander Kenshin himself from the core of his ranks. In the midst of this, the enemy Koshu army rallied. If you sympathize with Kenshin's mind prepared for certain tragedy, you cannot help but shed a few tears of sadness for his grudge. But if a broad view is taken of both sides, the battle would be evenhanded with a conspiracy of no winner or loser."

In addition to Ota Sukemasa's military assessment, in the future when Tokugawa Ieyasu was in Sunpu, it is said one of his first acts was to gather senior soldiers like Yokota Jinemon and Hirose Mino, both Koshu samurai, to evaluate Kawanakajima.

They told Ieyasu this.

"Because that battle will come to mark the division of the rise and fall for both Koshu and Echigo, it can be said to be natural for both to be cautious without moving lightly. Nevertheless, Shingen was a little too cautious. Kenshin formed battle lines that deliberately risked his life by placing his base on the dangerous ground of Mount Saijo. In contrast, Shingen realized he had outsmarted himself. From midnight to daybreak on September 9, if Kenshin established a plan to descend Mount Saijo and crossed the river to strike, perhaps, the main strength of the Echigo force would have been certainly devastated at Chikuma River. Pushing him out to Hachimanbara and striking his opponent at the rear after he stepped onto the plain was a blunder not fitting Shingen. In short, Shingen saw Kenshin's force and but missed seeing the motives of the commander Kenshin."

Scholars of military science held a variety of opinions, but, in general, have said nearly all there is to say in their criticisms of Sukemasa and Ieyasu.

Seen through modern eyes, Shingen looked out through physical substance and expert common sense. To the end, Kenshin surpassed his enemy's common sense and stimulated his sensitive mind unable to conceive ideas through theory or common sense and fought his very best in this battle.

If Kenshin were prudent and possessed a guarded common sense like Shingen and then took his army to Kawanakajima, his judgment would have been that it was impossible to attain the glory of being Uesugi of Echigo given the situation before the battle. What would his reputation be? To Kenshin, a military strategy with one true path was nothing other than glorious war. In short, the defense of his country, his advance, and his belief in returning home were one.

He was consumed by the words,

> In dying there is life.
>
> In living there is no life.

84
SOMETHING LEFT BEHIND

"DEN'E. DEN'EMON," SHINGEN called out. They were on the march back to Kofu.

Hajikano Den'emon turned his horse out of the line of hatamoto. He wondered why he was summoned as he approached Shingen's side.

Shingen nodded and said, "Good, I just remembered I left something on the battlefield. Now, what to do? You will quickly go back and return with it."

"Left something. ... What did you forget?"

"It's a sweet object. A young girl, not yet twenty years old, dressed in traveling clothes. She went astray amid the arrows and bullets. I ordered a soldier to place her safely in the priest's house at the shrine in Hachimanbara. Hurry back, see that she's safe, and return. No, pick her up and come back with her."

"Thank you for asking me.... I may find her soon. This fortunate man appreciates your kind words."

"No objection will be raised to your delayed return to Kofu. Your return with her will be the triumph."

The huge army left him and kept going forward to Kofu.

Den'emon was moved to tears at being favored on his journey back to the day's battlefield.

On the rainy night, blood soaking the earth was washed clean. In the unpopular night fog and morning fog over several days, the buds and flowers trampled into the grass were all alive and rising again.

Hajikano Den'emon tied his horse outside the forest in Hachimanbara. He noticed traces of raking inside the compound of the shrine like someone had swept it clean. The remains of the bloodbath and the chaos had also been raked. He could only see scarlet-tinted ivy and the blue darkness of cedar trees in the solitude.

Den'emon walked behind the shrine house. The daughter of the chief priest was washing diapers near the well in his memory of drawing water the other day.

"What?"

When the priest's daughter casually turned and saw Den'emon, she jumped with wet hands as if she collided at some time with the terror of a raging battle. Her complexion paled to an extreme.

Aware of his demeanor, Den'emon asked using particularly gentle words, "Your family has been taking care of a young woman named Tsuruna. I am a relative of hers. I am Den'emon of Kofu and have come to get her. Didn't she tell you?"

"Yes.... Of course."

As she dried her hands, the priest's daughter backed away from him and rushed inside through the kitchen door.

Inside the house, Tsuruna called out. She had not yet healed from the bullet wound and lay on her side on the bed. When she heard her father Den'emon had come, she rolled herself out to the open veranda.

"Father!"

Today, Den'emon did not have the fearsome look of the other day. He walked right over to her and silently wrapped his arms around this sweet thing.

"Tsuruna. Tsuruna ..." were the only words he said over and over.

Like no one else was around, the father and daughter embraced. As the priest's daughter watched from inside, she shyly revealed her bosom to feed her child.

85

THE ROAD BETWEEN RIVALS

THE NEXT DAY, the father Hajikano Den'emon and his daughter rode on
one horse along what is called Shingen's Boumichi Road to Kofu.

Although still dressed in full armor, with his lord's permission, Den'emon
was now only Tsuruna's father.

More than being given a castle or receiving a district, he felt he had
received the highest favor of the lord.

"Tsuruna."

"Yes."

"Do you remember your mother's face?"

"No."

"Your aunt?"

"Yes, I remember her."

"Your younger brothers?"

"A little …"

"Are you mad at your heartless parents?"

"Not at all. I simply hoped the war would be won soon so I could return
to your side."

"Now, you have returned to your father's side."

"When do I have to go back to Echigo?"

"It's all right. This time you'll go to your marital home."

The trip was unhurried. Time passed deep into autumn. Tsuruna felt like
she was in a dream. As they finally neared Kofu, they came across a group of
travelers coming from that direction.

"Oh!?" said Tsuruna and clung to her father's back. They were one on the
horse's back. Only she was unable to flee and hide.

"Tsuruna, what are you afraid of?" asked Den'emon as he turned and
pulled the reins to stop. Like a frightened bush warbler, she flinched slightly.

"Everyone in that crowd coming our way is an Echigo samurai. Kurokawa

Osumi-sama is one of them. Osumi-sama was my master. Until yesterday, he raised me as his child. What should I do?"

"Oh, I see," said Den'emon as he looked warily in their direction.

"The two on horseback look like Osumi and Saito Shimotsuke. The rest appear to be Echigo men captured during the battle led by Echigo envoys and are on their way to Kofu. But why are they coming this way?"

For a few moments, slightly suspicious, the group halted, only the ten men in front approached Den'emon.

"Oh, aren't you Lord Hajikano?" came an energetic voice in front. Without a doubt, he was the one-eyed envoy Saito Shimotsuke. His assistant envoy Kurokawa Osumi and his attendants accompanied him.

"Ah, Shimotsuke?"

The horses from both sides huddled together, and the men began to talk like old friends.

"This group had been arrested and later jailed in Kofu. Why are you here?" asked Den'emon.

"You see, I was given a note from Lord Shingen, and we easily passed through all barriers and checkpoints. We are in no way fugitives on the run after a jailbreak," said Shimotsuke.

"From the beginning, none of this is possible without Shingen's permission, but I don't understand all of you being freed unconditionally after the lord returned. Why did he allow you to leave?"

"Ha, ha, ha," roared Saito Shimotsuke in his usual tone and said, "The lord said this battle was over for now. There was no point in keeping us in a Kofu prison to live off of him. That being said, why not kill us? If ten or so accomplices of Kofu's spies on Echigo's list or Lord Shingen are arrested, they can be beheaded at any time and compensation requested. The lord who is expected to be wise and not blunder cut the ropes binding us yesterday and gave us this note. Because we were freed to return to our home country, the Koshu clan members imprisoned on Mount Kasuga were released without incident and left. In other words, he proposed an exchange of the lives of the enemies for those of the allies. At first, we didn't particularly want to live but were stumped on how to flatly refuse this considerate help. We were already on our way home to Echigo around the time the battle was winding down."

"I understand. Now, return home safely and be happy."

"You battled in Kawanakajima and after a long absence will return home with your daughter. Isn't that another reason to celebrate?"

"It's as you have guessed. For my daughter, I thank Kurokawa Osumi."

They exchanged bows. The pair returning to Kofu and the party returning to Echigo crossed paths on the road going east to west. Tsuruna waited for them to pass, after a few moments, she turned to see Kurokawa Osumi looking back at her. While personally feeling deep friendship and obligation, somehow, the farewells in this parting on Boumichi Road between warring states were not awkwardly exchanged. In the silence on that day with no fighting, "He is from Echigo" and "He is a Koshu samurai" were heard. Regardless of the clear distinction of the countries, the wish was to live and die in one's country.

86

AN AUTUMN MEMORIAL SERVICE

BELLFLOWERS FADED, AND Eulalia grass grew.

Saito Shimotsuke's party passed down through Kawanakajima and pointed their horses to Hokkoku Kaido Road.

The white walls of Kaizu Castle were visible from the Chikuma River. A portion of the Koshu army seemed to fill the area. As if to ask where was the battle, the shape of the castle and the appearance of the mountains and rivers were drenched in the light of peace.

"The number of men killed on the Koshu side exceeded 4,600. The number on the Uesugi side was as high as 3,470. Ah ... a great sacrifice."

Kurokawa Osumi was overcome by emotion. It's not certain, but news of the war and the wounded of both armies rapidly passed down the road. The party reached here already knowing every detail.

The parting of the gurgling waters of the Chikuma flowed nearby. Where had the allies fought desperately in the great battle over the past few days? Where had the many faces remembered of friends, relatives, and someone else's brother from home fought or died in battle?

Upon reflection, when the sun sets will be forgotten. Saito Shimotsuke made the steadfast vow.

"The three thousand lives whose bones are buried here did not die in vain,"

Seemingly unable to bear being there, he rushed to mount his horse and called to his companions.

"Let's go. The sun's already setting.... I'm off."

His companions had scattered over the plain. When he looked around at those shadows, one was stacking rocks to build a tower; another gathered the scattered pieces of armor or helmet visors and cut flowers for a memorial service. They abruptly turned, abandoned the rocks and flowers to run toward Saito Shimotsuke's horse.

87
A QUIET NIGHT

SOMEONE'S SECOND SON met the expected fine death.

Did the lord of that clan also take some incomparable action and achieve a splendid death in battle?

The family members left behind were probably proud. Their knowledge of their deeds could be inferred. Others wished to take their places in the next war.

When men gathered in the castle town of Kasugayama, that opinion was spoken for some time after the battle in Kawanakajima.

Everyday someone left his home and walked to a burial service in the field of warriors who died in battle or made a condolence call to a bereaved family.

For a time, more than three thousand came from the narrow country of Echigo. This post-war phenomenon took place in other towns in addition to the castle town of Kasugayama. Whether going to a village or going to a hamlet in the mountains, the smell of burning incense hung in the air. The bells of many temples rang everyday.

Uesugi Kenshin divined the day and held a large memorial service in Rinsenji Temple in the castle town.

Of course, on this day, the twenty-four generals and the entire clan on Mount Kasuga attended. The honored old and young members of the grieving family of a low-ranking foot soldier were seated in the courtyard to listen to Kenshin's kind words.

Kenshin returned to the castle when evening came.

As always, he sat alone facing the garden in the late autumn evening.

The candles were brought.

Usually, the candle position was not off by even one eye of the tatami. This is the act of a page trained with strict discipline.

He had no wife. His evening meal was simple like that of a Zen priest. When finished, he went right back to the living room. That room had no seats for merrymaking. When he returned here to sit, he always returned alone. Was he meditating or reading or, in rare instances, writing?

"… Who is it?"

He looked back. The sliding door of the annex room opened quietly. Someone entered, turned around, and closed the door. Kenshin remembered instantly.

"Yoshikiyo?"

When the candle was brought that evening, the page told him that Murakami Yoshikiyo was determined to see him that night and asked in confidence. Kenshin forgot he said for him to come at any time.

"Excuse me for disturbing you."

Yoshikiyo fell prostrate at a distance and stealthily looked in the direction of the candle.

When Kenshin sat quietly alone in the living room, Yoshikiyo heard he was always in Zen meditation, so this night he hesitated out of respect.

Surprisingly, however, Kenshin was reading *The Collection of Poems of Ancient and Modern Times* and the poetry writings beside him.

"No, not at all. Please come in."

Kenshin called a page and offered him a cushion. It had been some time since Murakami Moshikiyo had taken part in the field headquarters of the Uesugi clan, but he was not a vassal but a guest. He was a so-called visiting general.

88

A POETIC TURN OF MIND

"**YOU'RE ABSORBED IN** your studies."

"No, I'm bored and received this truly amusing calligraphy."

"They appear to be poems."

"They are ancient and modern poems, a gift from Konoe Sakitsugu. I don't think about reciting poetry, but I want to possess the mind of a poet amid the chaos of soldiers and horses."

"You say the mind of a poet."

"Well, what else is there to say? ... If I say the mind of Yamato, it's similar to the spirit. To say it more simply, flexible versus rigid, loving versus killing, eternal versus momentary, stillness versus motion."

"Wars year after year and day after day. A natural mind becomes the only way. However, when the war is thought to be never-ending, like going a long distance, like climbing a tall mountain, I believe examining the breath is critical. Exhale, inhale, hold for a long time. Breathe without disturbance. Think deeply. That is crucial."

"Yesterday, a lone horseman galloped into Shingen's central force. Today, on this still night, could that thought be embraced?

"For example, the string of a koto is plucked, but the sound diminishes. And except when a bow is shot, the string is removed.

"If removed, playing without them is forgotten. If played, their removal is forgotten. Reversing one's thoughts is hard.

"I can only put it this way. If we were ordinary men, at dawn, we see soldiers and horses and become familiar with writing as the light. I want a poetic mind in my blood. Simply put, both scholarship and martial arts are carried in one body. This is extremely easy but difficult, but it will happen.... Ha, ha, ha."

Kenshin smiled cheerfully under the lantern light. The attentive page occasionally picked up a barley sweet to offer to him and filled his tea. Finally, he asked, "What on earth happened tonight? Please tell me, Yoshikiyo, your complexion doesn't look good. What has happened?"

89
A BIRD IN DISTRESS

YOSHIKIYO'S HEAD DROPPED and tears fell.

"..."

The light shined on the heavy silence of the guest. Babbling water in the spring accompanying the quiet of the garden dampened the light. From time to time, leaves hit the canopy of the large palace bringing a rain shower to mind.

"I've pondered this matter. I have a favor to ask of you. It's extremely selfish of me, but please listen," Yoshikiyo said while prostrate. He seemed to be crying.

Nothing entered Kenshin's thoughts. He tilted his head and listened, but asked Yoshikiyo again what was his request.

Yoshikiyo wiped away his tears. He finally composed himself and respectfully thanked Kenshin for his hospitality until that day then he spoke.

"Somehow, I'd like to cancel one condition of my request to this clan nine years ago. Just today, I'd like to stop being chivalrous to the Murakami clan. I also request permission to leave and seclude myself in the mountains of Takano."

With extraordinary courage, Yoshikiyo said all of this in one breath. For this man who by nature had the reserve of a good man to make such a request, he probably pledged with exceptional determination and courage in his heart, and his feelings were honestly accepted.

"I see," said Kenshin staring in wide-eyed astonishment at him, "... Well, what can I say? Are you saying that you have given up on returning to the land of your ancestors, the former territory of Shinano, and the hope of again seeing its people as before?"

"Yes.... Over the last nine years until today, starting with the lord, I have been helped by the entire population of Echigo."

To say that broke Yoshikiyo's heart. His hands dropped down to the tatami and were covered by his head.

His hair shook. White frost was visible in his hair.

Now, he would become the guest of another clan and humbled himself before Kenshin but virtue flowed in this man's blood. He was a descendant of Seiwa Genji, a famous clan in Shinano. Kenshin immediately thought of how unfortunate this situation was when he saw that sign of aging. Half of his crime was remembering his responsibility to himself.

More than ten years ago, the Murakami clan was given authority over the entirety of northern Shinano. Centered on Katsurao Castle in Sakaki Prefecture, as a descendant in a family having the ancestor and local deity Shogun Minamoto no Yoriyoshi, anyone would shine in this esteemed position.

Because this occurred in the middle of the Tenbun era (1532-1555), year by year, this territory was being encroached on by the Takeda clan of Kai Province and ended in the Battle of Uedahara in its last days. Its appalling extinction, which would have been impossible if the world were at peace, was reported. The castle failed. The family scattered. His wife was said to have ended it all by throwing herself into the Chikuma River.

In August of year 22 of Tenbun (1553),

Yoshikiyo escaped from the defeated army nearly alone and came to Echigo and clung to Kenshin.

"Please help."

At that time, Kenshin was older than twenty. He seemed to look coldly at the figure with bowed knees making an honorable appeal about the end of this illustrious family.

"All right. Calm down."

Kenshin said yes. His was a small country on the frontier. It had few warriors and horses and began as a northern country with poor industry. Each year, Kenshin pulled the clouds of war and confronted the powerful Takeda clan in Koshu. In fact, this distressed bird with one wing entering Echigo was the beginning. It was an opportunity. The conflict between Kenshin and Shingen began here. People in the world at large, those of Echigo, and even those of Koshu widely held this belief.

Thus, a war started by a sliver of chivalry extended for a long nine years until today.

Moreover, the enemy nation was strong. The famous general Takeda Shingen was a courageous general of Kai shouting at the elite warriors and horses and counted on by many people in the world.

Still, Yoshikiyo's request had not been fulfilled. In the old fief of Yoshikiyo, as before, Takeda's invasion took pride in great violence. Was this to become an eternal circumstance? In the last few years, Yoshikiyo had given up his dream of returning to the land of his ancestors as nothing more than a fleeting wish.

Today, we will go there.

Yoshikiyo's heart had been acutely tormented at the huge memorial service held at Rinsenji Temple.

90
THE ANGUISHED YOSHIKIYO

OF COURSE, YOSHIKIYO attended the large memorial service held today.

His eyes saw the many bereaved families of the men killed in battle at Kawanakajima.

He saw the elderly mothers and fathers, the ashen-faced wives hugging young children and babies who no longer had fathers, the nephews, the uncles, the nieces, and numerous other related people in the courtyard today.

While a mountain of virtue in the human forms of Tenshitsu, Souken, and a multitude of priests and monks lifted the largest Buddhist scripture of the Zen sect and prayed for the happiness of the departed souls in the other world, Yoshikiyo was unable to raise his eyes to look up at the altar. He averted his eyes and could not look at the many grieving families filling the corridor and the stairs of the Buddhist temple.

He questioned himself, blamed himself, and found it all unbearable.

"In the end, I lived to escape to Echigo."

In an instant, he was gripped by guilt, bells rang in his ears. He thought the souls of more than three thousand war dead were shouting to reproach him. Yoshikiyo had no will to live.

He already made his decision while in Rinsenji Temple. He would shave his head and enter the priesthood. He would escape from the world of struggle, prosperity, and decline. At the same time, he threw away his hopes and dreams of returning just one time to Eimon, washed away his attachments, expressed thanks for the long patronage of the Uesugi clan to escape the world and hide in the high plains.

If so, this terrible sacrifice would not occur a second time. A lifetime of fervent praying for the happiness of the deceased in the other world would be compensation for what had happened. He would enter the priesthood to apologize.

"… That is what I think. Until today, I thought like a traveler wandering alone. Even in death, I will never forget my great debt for your patronage year after year through huge military expense and the precious blood of officers and soldiers. More than that, I've caused many lives to be lost and brought grief to the many people left behind. I do not know how to apologize for this. Even if I returned to the land of my ancestors, there is no joy when alone. I have no words, but may your compassion somehow forgive my self-indulgence."

Yoshikiyo's genuine feelings flowed without a break from his heart.

Kenshin lightly closed his eyes for a short time to listen. However, when Yoshikiyo finished the long explanation of his anguish, Kenshin opened fiery eyes.

"Silence.... Yoshikiyo, please stop talking."

Kenshin spoke quietly.

In fact, however, the tone of his voice was as if a huge rock pressed on him from the beginning.

91

ENLIGHTENMENT FOR ONE
AND ENLIGHTENMENT FOR ALL

"Yes.... Yes."

Yoshikiyo trembled unknowingly.

Anyone would say that the ordinary Kenshin was entirely feminine. This was the first time in nine years he faced eyes so frightening on the tatami before that man.

Kenshin was not infuriated. He did not roar or rave. Somehow in a quiet voice, anger would swell. He was enraged.

"What are you saying? What are you saying? If you'll be quiet and listen, you seem to understand that thing you call war as a curiosity of man or a diversion of the bored."

"Is th... that absurd? This unworthy man did not make light of the hardship of war. I thoroughly understood the misery of war to the marrow of my bones."

"Silence!"

"Yes ..."

"As you age, don't move your tongue with foolish mischief. War is not as simple as the understanding of one Murakami Yoshikiyo as the pursuit of a small country. Its meaning is not that small. I infer from your words that you did no more than pass through the middle of a war. You still don't seem to understand what a real war is."

"That's ... that's probably true."

"You look confused. First, you have doubts about what is a real war. I should laugh. Were you under the impression that a modicum of chivalry in response your request was the reason I fought bloody wars with Shingen over nine years?... Why? Why?"

Kenshin made no sound but his shoulders shook with laughter. He followed with these impressive words.

"Please think. For over one hundred years since the Onin era, the Ankoku of Udai was a powerful clan with influence over various lands, the self-awakening was slow in coming but began with Tokugawa and Oda in Tokai and Mori and Ouchi in Saikai and understood by Shingen in Kai, Kenshin here, Hojo in Sagami, and for a short time by Imagawa of Sakai in Sun'en. Actions in Japan today are changing like a riptide and reflect a swift revolution. Within the tide of this age, the problems are not somehow becoming a famous family in Shinano, and whether Murakami Yoshikiyo will go to ruin or flourish or die or live. This was nothing more than a single straw drifting on the vast sea of actions in Japan."

He put particular emphasis on his final words.

Yoshikiyo blanched. The blush was gone from his thin earlobes as he listened intently.

Kenshin continued, "If I ask myself why have I fought Shingen for so many years, originally, there was my belief in myself. I turned twenty-three and, first, prepared for the task of pacifying the nation internally, and that reached the ears of the slightly intoxicated emperor who granted me a court rank. While I humbly sat at a distance and never having had even an audience before the emperor, I received the favor of the gracious emperor. The extreme of irreverence, that is, I will go to the capital next year at all costs, lie prone before the emperor, bow at an intimate distance, and be given the emperor's gift cup.... In fact, it was the time I knew the joy created in my body by holding a bow and arrow. The importance of fighting is the nobility of fighting as long as I'm alive on this land. I will fight. I will fight. At the same time, I was deeply impressed, my heart was penetrated, and would give my life to protect a clan of a certain standing. Without regrets, I took this vow deep into my heart."

"..."

"Since then, I've used no other bow and arrow. In the early summer of Eiroku year 2, I went to the capital again. Before that time, the emperor graciously gave this order to me. If there are disturbances at the border, you should attack and bring order to imperial lands. If a violent country hurts the people, go and pacify. That was the emperor's message and more than what my incompetent self deserved. As a vassal, I will not state my response to the emperor's consideration. However, even in this far-off corner of Hokuetsu, I have not forgotten that gracious imperial message for one day. Not to mention, on days the soldiers move ..."

It rained that night. The rainfall was accompanied by the splashing sounds of water overflowing the gutter and landing under the eaves.

Kenshin, who had no wife, resembled a Zen priest wearing a pilgrim's half-length haori coat and a greenish-brown hood. When he fiercely spouted his true feelings about this problem, his eyes were actually young. Sometimes his tears flowed with Yoshikiyo's. However, Yoshikiyo's eyes were drowned in the anguish of the small love of his own enlightenment. As his eyes filled with tears resembling the sea of enlightenment of oneself and the world, he looked up and tightly embraced a promising future and a warm heart.

92

WIND AND RAIN HITTING
THE WINDOW LAST NIGHT

"**FOR THE FIRST** time tonight, I questioned your motives. Looking at my small ambition and shortcomings, I feel nothing but shame.... You have listened to the troubles of an unnecessary, insignificant man who has disturbed you on this quiet night. Forgive me," said Yoshikiyo.

His apology was from the heart.

At last, he fully realized the aim and the meaning of the war that was molded by Kenshin and enlightened his ignorant mind.

When he understood, Yoshikiyo no longer wanted to be embarrassed by thoughts of the battles year after year with Koshu started for the sake of Murakami Yoshikiyo and wanted to erase them.

Kenshin softened his words.

"No, I erupted with harsh words without thinking this evening. To tell you the truth, the clan's vassals nurtured over the years and over three thousand cherished men were lost in this great battle at Kawanakajima. Privately, I'm having difficulty healing my melancholy. No, more than you, more than anyone, I berate myself over my deep responsibility and sorrow. More so on evenings like this, a gentle, rainy night after the battle."

Kenshin fixed his eyes on the lamplight and was about to continue, but pity for Yoshikiyo's tragic heart stopped him. He did not want his words to turn into meaningless chatter.

Then Kenshin said, "… Imagine what's in my heart."

"I understand. I do."

"If you do, in the end, the dead bodies piled on the battlefield, this country of Echigo, the wives with no husbands, and the children with no fathers would not be satisfied by the explanation that this was all the fault of a single man. Don't be so small-minded to think this was for one man. More than that, in your one life, in my one life, while we're breathing, we will pray for some major offering to the people of the capital in the mornings and the evenings for all time."

That ended the talk that night. However, Murakami Yoshikiyo returned to his residence and thought about Kenshin's words the rest of the night and came to appreciate his mind. Like ten years were somehow forgotten, he fell into a pleasant, peaceful sleep.

Until this day, he simply thought of war as appalling, violent, painful, and demanding sacrifice, but it suddenly had great meaning. He realized that in war the present husk of evil is cast off, then comes rebuilding, and all the land in Japan left unplowed because of war is plowed again. Also, the blood that flowed and the bones buried in war are united in the work of loyalty.

After that, Yoshikiyo peacefully snored in his sleep and awoke with a light heart. On another day of fighting, it's said he serenely stood at the lead and grew braver after turning fifty.

93
A NOBLE CAUSE
AND A MAGNANIMOUS ACT

AFTER THE GREAT battle in Kawanakajima, another event revealed the big heart of Kenshin. The party of Uesugi envoys captured in Koshu like Saito Shimono and Kurokawa Osumi returned safely to Echigo through the tolerance of Shingen.

In response to his tolerance, of course, Kenshin rapidly carried out his own generous policy. Several tens of spies from Koshu imprisoned in his country were brought to the castle town of Kasugayama.

"All of you received your lord's orders, scattered here in Echigo, but in vain because you were arrested. Now, you will be returned home after only seeing the inside of a jail. That may be shameful to your lord. Your relatives and friends would also be ashamed. There is nothing that could be called a fortress at Echigo's front. It will be nice for you to see places here and there in Echigo you may have wished to see."

Sent from the magistrate and accompanied by government officials, they were divided into several groups and were guided to see a few places over the three days and finally given traveling expenses and sent back to their country.

"Shingen displayed charity to our envoys. They had gone to Koshu as honorable envoys. All those released in Echigo were incorrigible enemy spies. This treatment seems too magnanimous."

This wasn't a criticism, but numerous voices in the clan were quite worried. All of the Koshu ruffians freed in Echigo quarreled.

"This is no good. I'll never be able to make my way into the castle town of Kasugayama a second time. For three days in broad daylight, I was walked through many places like that. Even the women of the castle town will surely recall this face. Even if disguised, I'll be discovered in no time."

Fear over Kenshin's generosity grew, and they couldn't scramble fast

208

enough back to Koshu.

Through this experience, they guessed that Kenshin's war was not a personal grudge or a self-serving invasion. Kenshin saw a citizen of Japan even in an enemy soldier. He was a soldier with an aesthetic sense. He took a philosophical view in which both enemy and ally will return to a larger life in this country where all blood flows together in the nation of Japan. These were the reasons for Kenshin's rebuke of the weakness in the spirit of Murakami Yoshikiyo and his heartfelt sympathy for the enemy ruffians.

However, Kenshin was a soldier. He vowed to win absolutely. Therefore, he did not conclude that handling enemy ruffians in this way was a foolish act that would result in disaster for the allies. Rather, the action taken by him would later strengthen the defense of Echigo.

His one-word orders and all his everyday actions until his death at forty-nine were designed to win battles.

To win, he will have to lose himself. By losing himself, he will be unable to realize his ideal. Loving himself, always being cautious, and caring for his health, a devoted man like him rarely became a military commander.

Thus, his ego was no ordinary one. His ego differed from one of self-interest and selfish desire. Kenshin was already not Kenshin alone but completely one with the country that gave him life. He upheld the model of a so-called man of the imperial court and a public figure.

He rapidly achieved great nobility within himself from his youth. Both times he went to the capital, he vowed to strengthen his conviction. At the age of twenty-four, he went to the far-off capital from the borderland of Echigo for an audience with the emperor. While hearing and seeing the dreary state of the Imperial Palace at that time, his young mind was struck by the obsolescence of the Court Council, the powerlessness of the shogunate, and the corruption of the public mind. His ambition gushed out like a spring. At that time the life of Uesugi Kenshin had already been decided.

94
THE BEAUTY OF THE MOUNTAINS
AND THE SEA

THE BATTLEFIELD WOULD change each year, but the war after Kawanakajima continued without end.

In Eiroku year 5 (1562), Shingen fought his way into Ueno; Kenshin went to battle in Numata in Joshu.

In the sixth year, he went to war in Kanto to assist Sano Castle. And the following year, he again set up camp at Kawanakajima.

This time, Shingen sent his army to Hida. In July of the eighth year, the Echigo force also entered Shinano to halt Shingen.

"Finally, Lord Long Legs of Koshu will stretch his legs and relax with the coming of age," Kenshin once joked, but Shingen's versatile actions foiled that prediction each year.

At last, the long legs of Lord Long Legs were bitten by enemies and, for once in his life, he raised his hands in despair.

From Eiroku year 11 (1568) to Genki year 1 (1570), these long years began life without salt. The entire country was attacked by salt.

The long-legged Shingen sent troops to Suruga and became the master bitten by his own dog by a grueling plan concocted by his enemies. The two clans of the Imagawa and the Hojo conspired to enact a strict delivery ban to Kai Province, Shinano Province, and a portion of Joshu.

"Not one cup of salt will enter any territory under Shingen's control."

The official announcement stated that anyone caught selling even a pinch of salt on the sly to the enemy would be beheaded.

They endured for six months to a year until all salt stores in the storehouses were exhausted. Through the mountains and the rivers, black-market dealings provided small quantities. However, as the third year approached, Shingen had been backed into a corner. He had not complained once over three years.

Day by day the worry etched deeper into his face.

"Is there nothing I can do?"

Here is the history. The Kai, Shinano, and Jomo regions depended on the domains of the Hojo and the Imagawa clans not only for salt but for all marine products. The hardship created was absolute. The skin of the fief's population acquired a visible blue tint. The number of sickly people soared. More than that, the inability to eat miso and pickled goods fatally threatened the peasants' lives. Thus, agricultural production declined, and morale was shaken. As expected, Kofu would do nothing other than self-destruct.

"Not yet? We can devastate Kofu in one stroke."

Rumors sprang from all quarters. Even on the Echigo front, some generals constantly urged Kenshin to act. But during that time, Kenshin didn't dare move his troops to Kai or Shinano.

Envoys also came from the Imagawa clan seeking an alliance on the salt ban policy. He pushed back by saying, "In this clan, particularly in this clan, if we were to establish that policy, it would be uncharitable."

However, Tokugawa Ieyasu in Mikawa concluded an alliance with Kai that year and did not permit an opening with Shingen.

In desperation, Shingen still sent troops to various provinces to acquire salt. They suddenly pushed into Uesugi's territory in Joshu. Unable to overlook that, Kenshin immediately crossed the Mikuni mountain range to repel them, then withdrew to Kofu and returned to Echigo.

Soon after returning, Kenshin summoned Kurata Gorozaemon, the Magistrate of the Storehouses, to give him an order.

"During this campaign, I heard about the lives of the people in the territories of Kai and Shinano. The rumor was salt has been cut off, and the suffering of the peasants is indescribable. Promptly send salt from the north sea by land and sea to Kai and Shinano."

Gorozaemon couldn't believe his ears. He was doubtful and to make sure, he asked, "To the enemy country?"

"Yes," said Kenshin with a huge nod. He added a warning.

"Originally, there was no reason to open the salt stores in the castle. I issued a decree to urge merchants to sell salt as fast as possible to salt merchants in Kai and Shinano. However, I fear they will take advantage of the shortage and profiteer. Strictly limit the price to Echigo prices and to no more than the average."

95
YOU AND I

SALT CROSSED THE provincial border and flowed in without limits.

The flush of life returned to the complexions of the peasants of Koshu. This reverberated in town after town. The merchants were excited and walked around portioning out the salt. The people seeing the salt grabbed handfuls of its whiteness.

"Thank you," they said through tears. They worshipped the salt and made offerings of salt at the altars of village shrines. The light offerings burned brightly.

In the castle in Tsutsujigasaki, Shingen heard a detailed account of this situation, and his eyes lit up.

"… Is that so?" was all he said. He voiced nothing about his approval, feelings, or criticism.

"…?"

Initially, he looked pained, followed by skepticism. During the last great battle in Eiroku year 4, Kenshin's strategy was to risk his life for others. Shingen's mind was engulfed by fog as he looked at Kenshin's incomprehensible encampment on Mount Saijo.

A letter arrived for him. Because Kenshin was on Mount Kasuga, Shingen was suspicious when he opened the letter. The letter was simple.

> Over time, you and I called out troops and responded with troops. The tools of our fight were bows and arrows. Our fighting hearts are different in design. My ideals are not your ideals. Your wishes are not my wishes. In other words, our confrontations over successive years borrowed a plain unequaled in this world for us to spread out our battle formations.
>
> Yet in battles between military clans, rice and salt are not

weapons. It is not necessary for you alone to have rice or salt, but they are the living expenses of the peasants. Because the peasants are righteous and the country is vast, they have no connection to the attacks. Anyone would detest the miserable plan and vile motive of the Imagawa clan of Suruga Province and the Hojo clan of Sagami Province.

This latest intent of mine is nothing other than to supply your country with salt through commerce with my country. If this wish concerns you, it will be withdrawn. Make the elite troops under your banner even better. We will not meet on the battlefield again.

"..."

Shingen read the letter three times. The mist in his eyes cleared. However, there was no question he held Kenshin in high esteem. His beautiful mind illuminated and enriched Shingen's spirit. He only felt breaths of pure heroism. The sense of winning or losing was transcended.

He reverently folded the letter and raised it to his head then stored it in the case beside him. This time, Shingen did not utter one word in excitement. He felt there were no words to be said.

96
THE SALT FESTIVAL

ECHIGO AND KAI during these three years were destined to be enemy countries. While firmly holding the border, their actions faced other directions.

From Genki year 3 (1572) to Tensho year 1 (1573), Shingen left for Mikatahara with Tokai in his sights, crushed the army of Tokugawa Ieyasu, and approached the main castle at Hamamatsu.

In August of the same year, Kenshin went on a pacification campaign in Etchu Province. The occupation near Mount Fuji ended in March, and he returned to Kasugayama Castle in April. Soon he received a shocking report.

"During March, Takeda Harunobu Nyudo Shingen of Kai passed away."

It's said Kenshin was having lunch when he heard the urgent news from a nearby vassal.

"What? Kai Nyudo has died? ... Ah, he was a fine rival over many years and to see him again on another day will never be?"

His hand holding the chopsticks dropped to his knee. He closed his eyes spilling bitter tears and muttered a caution to vassals on fighting morale.

"A country without an enemy will go to ruin. Or the bows and arrows of Echigo may go limp. With a genius like Shingen as my enemy, the objectives I always cultivated of being defeated by him and defeating him are gone from this world. How regrettable. A tragedy."

One of his generals heard the report of his death and said, "The time is perfect. The seasoned warriors of the clan in Kofu will certainly sink to the depths of destruction as if the lamplight has been lost. If we took a large force on a campaign, his entire territory would be easily upset."

Several approached Kenshin to explain their plans. He laughed.

"Stop it! Stop it! This will only seek out the contempt of the entire country. If we entered Koshu to overthrow them the morning after his death, the mourning of the death of their pillar Shingen would be inadequate.

However, in three years, Kofu will be an impregnable fortress as before. Three years from now, who knows?"

Later, Kenshin dispatched senior vassals to Kaizu Castle to mourn Shingen's death with sympathy.

After the envoy returned from the condolence call, the facts of Shingen's death became known in detail. Just as one thought, his death was a fitting death. All of his posthumous plans were stated in his will to the generals of the field headquarters and his clan. He favored the position in Kai and not to allow a rapid decline in its strength.

Shingen's illness began during the siege of Hamamatsu Castle and the soldiers finally began to approach Mikawa. His sudden death at this precise moment gave rise to various opinions, and some provinces looked on with skepticism. The encirclement of Noda Castle was released. He fell seriously ill during the fast return to Kofu. When he reached the Tsutsujigasaki Yakata residence, he had already died.

When he faced death, he called his son and heir Nobukatsu, Katsuyori, other clan members, and his generals to his bedside.

"After I die, do not move the soldiers without cause. In particular, I trust you will trust Kenshin in the neighboring province who will not betray me."

His will included this request:

> Return my skin and bones to the depths.
> Elegance without blush painted on.

They say his breath stopped when his trembling hand finished writing his final *gatha* verse.

From the time he fell ill until he died, he wrote his seal on eight hundred sheets of paper. The purpose was to make the world think Shingen had not died although he was gone. He prepared with all his heart for their possible use in the distant future.

Only a hero knows a hero's mind. It was not beyond Kenshin's imagination. As he said, for three years after Shingen's death, the Takeda clan with its Kai Genji ancestry would influence the surrounding territories and not show any failure.

However, one time, they went to Nagashino and suffered a crushing defeat when intercepted by the forces of Oda Nobunaga and Tokugawa Ieyasu, deteriorated, and swiftly retreated to the position in Kai. As expected, the elite troops continued to lose face.

Under these circumstances, the vicissitudes of life also came to Kenshin. Five years after Shingen's death, Kenshin abruptly left this world. The sudden deaths of both men were mystifying and believed to be destiny.

Ordinarily, Kenshin was robust and healthy but enjoyed sake. Later remembering how regularly he enjoyed a cup while on horseback brought tears to his grieving family and vassals. To this day, incredibly large cups like ordinary sake cups are left at Uesugi's shrine. It's not difficult to imagine a single pickled plum as a distasteful side dish after easily drinking a keg of sake.

Surely long ago
I returned from every direction.
The conquest reversed.
A thousand generations of white snow.

This was an old composition of his. One snowy night when he went to the capital as a young man, he recited the beginning during a meeting with General Yoshiteru.

Approaching the beauty of the one color of snow, the spirit of revival embraced by his heart was already blowing at this time. More than snow, a glimpse of the pure nation leaked out.

Ashikaga Yoshiteru, the 13th shogun, was a youthful general at nineteen. As expected, Kenshin didn't know whether to assimilate his ideals. However, Kenshin did not change his bonds of friendship even after the unnatural death of Yoshiteru and the next generation Yoshiaki became the shogun. A great force had lent this man to secretly save the Muromachi shogunate from collapse.

To gain the advantage, he confronted Nobunaga who was the destroyer in full opposition to him. The inevitable clash was a bitter fight fought by diplomats and warriors.

CREDITS

Japanese source text:
Aozora Bunko.
Yoshikawa, Eiji. 上杉謙信 (*Uesugi Kenshin*), Shunkan Asahi, January 4 to May 24, 1942.
Accessed March 7, 2014.
https://www.aozora.gr.jp/cards/001562/card56461.html

Front cover image:
National Diet Library Digital Collections.
Tsukioka, Yoshitoshi. 芳年武者无類弾正少弼上杉謙信入道輝虎
(*Yoshitoshi's Courageous Warriors: Danjo Daihitsu Uesugi Kenshin Nyudo Kagetora*),
武者无類外二三枚続キ画帖 (*Musha Burui Hokani Sanmai Tsudzuki Gajoku*),
1883.
Accessed February 2, 2019.
http://dl.ndl.go.jp/info:ndljp/pid/1302830

Back cover map, Kenshin's dragon kanji and Bishamonten kanji:
National Diet Library Digital Collections.
Nagano-shi Kyoikukai. 川中嶋戦史 (*A History of the Battle of Kawanakajima*),
Nagano-shi Kyoikukai, 1928 (in Japanese).
Accessed March 20, 2019.
http://dl.ndl.go.jp/info:ndljp/pid/1187342

Back cover woodblock print:
National Diet Library Digital Collections.
Ichiyusai Kuniyoshi (aka Utagawa Kuniyoshi). 武田上杉川中嶋大合戦の図
(Frames 2 and 3 of triptych of Takeda and Uesugi at the Battle of Kawanakajima).
Accessed April 2, 2019.
http://dl.ndl.go.jp/info:ndljp/pid/1305638

ABOUT THE AUTHOR

Yoshikawa Eiji (August 11, 1892 - September 7, 1962) was a Japanese novelist and master of the historical novel. He was born Yoshikawa Hidetsugu in Yokohama, Japan. His father Yoshikawa Naohiro was a former samurai in the Odawara clan. After working at a variety of jobs, he gained fame as a popular writer with the serial publication of the novel *Naruto Hicho* [The Secret Record of Naruto] in *Osaka Mainichi Shimbun* (August 11, 1926 - October 14, 1927). He gained a wider following with *Miyamoto Musashi*, published serially beginning in 1935. A prolific author, he received the Order of Culture in 1960 and the third Mainichi Geijutsu art prize in 1961. In his honor, The Yoshikawa Eiji Prize for Literature was established in 1967 and The Yoshikawa Eiji Prize for New Writers in 1980.

From the Japanese Wikipedia page for Eiji Yoshikawa (https://ja.wikipedia.org/wiki/吉川英治) (Accessed February 6, 2019)

www.jpopbooks.com

Made in United States
North Haven, CT
28 July 2023

39647360R00138